Jacob's Well

Brenda Hall

Jacob's Well is a work of fiction inspired by the story of the Samaritan Woman in St John's Gospel 4: 1-30

ISBN: 978-1-291-50096-7

Copyright © 2013 Brenda Hall

All rights reserved, including the right to reproduce this book, or portions thereof in any form. No part of this text may be reproduced, transmitted, downloaded, decompiled, reverse engineered, or stored, in any form or introduced into any information storage and retrieval system, in any form or by any means, whether electronic or mechanical without the express written permission of the author.

This is a work of fiction. Names and characters are the product of the author's imagination - other than Jesus - and any resemblance to actual persons, living or dead, is entirely coincidental.

PublishNation, London
www.publishnation.co.uk

For Tony, Richard, Stephen,
Mandy, Ben and Amy

'There are three things that last: faith, hope and love and the greatest of these is love.'

1 Corinthians 13:13

Chapter One

It was the fifteenth year of the reign of Tiberius Caesar in Roman occupied Palestine, where the hill country region of Samaria lay between Judea to the south and Galilee to the north. Bordering the land to the west, was the Great Sea, its shimmering turquoise waters crested with the billowing sails of trading ships, ploughing their way to Egypt, Greece and Rome. To the east, the fertile plains and valleys stretched towards the mountains and the village at Sychar that nestled in their shadow.

Behind the walls of the city of Sebaste, built on a hill in central Samaria, the household of Marcus Gallius Marcellus, a Roman nobleman of equestrian rank, was beginning to stir. From the courtyard, the hushed voices of the house slaves, talking together as they cleared away the remains of the previous nights feasting, reached Leah as she stood wide awake and watchful at the bedroom window.

She was a strikingly graceful woman, although no longer beautiful. The puckered red scar running down the side of her face from her temple to beneath her left ear had taken care of that. Even so, the steady mesmerizing gaze of her tawny-gold, upward slanting eyes still held the power to disturb and attract in equal measure.

As the dawn sun cast a shaft of light across the room it dazzled her with its brightness and for a lingering moment she watched the dust motes dancing in its beam. Then she closed her eyes and clenched her hands, until her nails bit deep into her palms, the skin stretching tight across her knuckles.

Dimly at first, and then louder, a rising chorus of squabbling birdsong began to penetrate her consciousness. Allowing her hands to relax she moved cautiously from the window. With slender fingers she tucked back a thick lock of hair that had fallen loose from beneath her veil and looked at Marcellus, lying sprawled across the wide bed, snoring softly.

His right arm lay coiled above his head with fist clenched in a gesture of menace even in sleep. His left, thrown outwards across the purple silk of the covers, rested with fingers curled innocently towards an upturned palm. As he grunted and shifted his position her eyes darkened from tawny gold to brown, the knowledge of the brutality he was capable of momentarily filling her with a fear that rendered her incapable of movement.

Leah had suffered at the hands of other men but for none had she felt the deep and conflicting emotions of hatred and pity that she did for Marcellus. A former tribune in the Roman army, he had suffered a sword thrust to his hip in battle that had signalled the end of his military career. Engulfed in bitterness and dangerously unstable, he was now driven by a fury and self-loathing so intense it threatened to consume them both.

It had been three years since he had bought her and her young son, Daniel, at a slave auction. Unaware that she was Daniel's mother he had put the boy to work in his stables and taken her as his concubine. All that he demanded she gave, whilst remaining aloof and unknowable, her determination not to reveal anything about herself fuelling his rage.

As she watched him she raised a hand to her face and touched the scar, tracing a path along its length with her finger. Bitterly she recalled that beautiful, temperate evening of almost a year ago, when he had arranged one of his lavish banquets, offering her as a prize for the guest still sober enough to be standing when the feasting and other entertainments were done. The cynical amusement of the men who pretended to be his friends had scarcely been concealed.

The sun was dipping low in the sky, blushing the marble statues pink with its dying rays as a young girl lit the oil lamps, shielding their wicks until the flames steadied and the garden became illuminated in a soft, buttery glow. Around the walls of the villa almond trees were showing off the last of their fading blossom, whilst below them camomile bushes frothed with small white flowers.

By the side of the wide, arched entrance a towering palm cast its shadow towards an ornately decorated table, on which baskets of honey sweetened cakes, freshly baked bread and bowls of fruit stood ready for serving.

Standing silent and watchful in the dark recesses prostitutes and young male slaves waited. Marcellus catered for every taste.

The large dining room, with its floors and walls decorated in intricately patterned mosaics, lay open to the still night air that hung heavy with the cloying smell of burning incense. Already well on their way to drunkenness, eight of the city's richest dignitaries sprawled comfortably on the couches, picking from the bowls of salad, olives and quail eggs that lay spread around the table.

As she walked towards them the rising tenor of their excited voices grated on her. Unaware of what Marcellus had planned for her, or of the ugliness to come, she took her seat beside him as platters piled with lamb, pork and fish, cooked in rich plum and pepper sauces, were carried out from the kitchen, and wine goblets refilled to the brim.

The raucous laughter of the guests was reaching a crescendo as Cato, a Roman aristocrat of dubious integrity, spat out an olive stone and rose from his seat. With a mocking smile he raised his hand, commanding their attention in his high-pitched patrician voice.

'Come, my friend,' he cried, as he turned towards Marcellus. 'Parade for us your charming concubine so we may all appreciate the prize that is on offer for one of us tonight.'

His cold, dead-fish eyes fixed on her, and only in that moment did she begin to guess what was meant to happen.

Marcellus stood and rocked back on his heels, his face mean and flushed with drink. Roughly he dragged her to her feet and clumsily gripped her harder in an effort to steady her as she stumbled. As she regained her footing she struggled to pull free and his hold on her tightened.

Then he released her abruptly, but not before she had felt the tremor that ran through his body and heard his sharp intake of breath. She followed his gaze to where a Roman centurion stood leaning against the palm tree, watching them, his face obscured in shadow. Feverishly, and without much hope, she silently willed him to join them because of his restraining influence on Marcellus. The two men stared at each other across the divide that separated them and then the soldier straightened up and left.

The frisson of excitement around the table was palpable, as the amused guests avidly absorbed the small drama that had been played out silently, in front of them. It was Porcius, the city's most prosperous trader in gold and silver, who was the first to speak. His small black eyes, sunk in the fleshy folds of his face, glinted with gleeful malice as he heaved himself up, raising his goblet high above his head.

'A toast to Varinius,' he shouted. 'The noble centurion, who considers himself above dining with the guests of his friend, Marcellus.'

He swayed unsteadily as he took a gulp of wine, then he fell back heavily onto the couch, a sly smile pulling at the corners of his mouth. The young male slave, who rushed forward with a wet cloth to wipe his hands and mop up the spillage, received a sharp cuff around the head for his trouble.

Marcellus's features had turned leaden and then paled and she caught again, as she had so many times before, the look of abject wretchedness behind his eyes that always threatened to confuse the hatred she felt for him.

Cato tipped out the two remaining quail eggs from a wooden bowl and banged it hard on the table, cutting through the shrieks of loud laughter and vulgarity that had followed Porcius's mockery. As the noise subsided he looked around slowly at each of them with an arrogant tilting of his chin.

'Let me tell you gentlemen, I shall be the only one this night remaining sober enough to claim the beautiful Leah.'

He spoke slowly, each word measured and threatening, his boast arousing a coarse lewdness in his fellow diners that filled her with a fear she knew he had noticed and relished. She was unaware that she had stopped breathing until she heard herself take a loud gasp of air. Marcellus stood clenching and unclenching his fists before roughly pushing her down hard onto her seat.

'It is over. She will not be anyone's prize,' he spat out savagely. 'It was a jest; never intended to be taken seriously.'

Cursing loudly he clapped his hands for the musicians and dancers to begin their entertainment and called for his goblet to be refilled. He raised it towards her, holding her eyes, before taking a long drink. She knew his hip had begun to pain him as she watched him walk awkwardly to where two prostitutes stood, smiling and waiting, their arms wrapped around each other.

Cato leaned towards her then, so close she could smell the perfume he had used and feel the heat from his body. With a delicate finger he traced a path down her arm and then gripped her wrist, hard. She cringed in revulsion and turned her head away, and his smile went cold as he released his hold on her.

'Rest assured,' he whispered, as he bent his head towards her, his lips almost touching her ear. 'Marcellus did offer you and I am determined you and I will be together later when he and the others lie drunk and snoring in their vomit. I am intrigued by the harlotry you practise that has him so in thrall to you, and which gives us all such entertainment to watch.'

Angered by what Marcellus had done, and by Cato's unconcealed lust, she was determined not to allow him to see her fear. With a supreme effort of will she regained her composure. As she turned to face him again she tilted her head to one side and looked deep into his eyes, allowing her lips to part into a soft smile. His sallow skin flushed with expectation.

'I would rather be taken into the Judean desert and left there to be eaten by the wild animals than have you touch me,' she mouthed softly as she held his gaze.

Briefly Cato's face contorted with a savage fury before relaxing into a contemptuous smile. Catching her again by her wrist and twisting hard, so that her skin burned, he pulled her closer, speaking so softly she had to strain to hear him.

'That, madam, can most certainly be arranged.'

His eyes bored into hers and his voice rose and hardened. The warning was stark.

'Be careful woman, I know many ways of causing pain without leaving a trace and I promise you, we will celebrate this night together.'

Much later he claimed her.

At dawn Marcellus arrived, dishevelled and raging, to drag her naked from the wide couch where Cato lay propped on one elbow, laughing in amusement, his expression avid for what was to come. As Marcellus pushed her down onto the floor she curled into a ball, shielding her face with her hands.

He raised the vine stick he was carrying and beat her until his arm ached and his breathing became laboured. Then he stopped and released his grip on the stick, allowing it to fall at his feet.

Wide-eyed and numbed with shock she lay on her side as he stared down at her. Silently he pressed his foot into her shoulder and pushed her gently onto her back. And the menace in his gentleness was terrifying. Slowly and deliberately he bent towards her until she could smell his stale breath, hot on her face. His voice was guttural.

'Perhaps, woman, if you were a little less attractive you might not be able to whore so freely.'

Brutally he grabbed a handful of her hair and yanked back her head. Unsheathing his dagger with his free hand, he pressed the tip into her temple. As the blood began to ooze, he drew it slowly down the side of her face.

'You belong to me whore. Don't ever forget it,' he said, wiping the blood from his dagger down the front of his toga before sheathing it again.

She wasn't aware of his foot drawing back until she felt the blow and heard her ribs crack. For a while he stood looking down on her, his face ashen and impassive. Then he turned and limped from the room.

Inch by inch she dragged herself across the floor to lean with her back against the wall, each agonising breath rasping in her throat as she pressed a hand to her face in an attempt to stem the flow of blood. Cato rolled over and slept. Much later Marcellus returned to drive him out. Through a thick tide of pain she watched him stroll towards the doorway where he paused to look back over his shoulder. With contemptuous indifference he raised a languid hand in farewell.

'Thank you, Marcellus, for a wonderful evening and for the extraordinary services of your concubine; you should have joined us,' he said, his high-pitched laughter echoing around the room as he left.

She closed her eyes, certain that Marcellus would follow and kill him. But he didn't. Instead, remorseful and self-pitying, he wrapped his cloak around her and lifted her into his arms to carry her to his bed. Gently he bathed her, and bound her ribs, before cleaning the blood-encrusted gash on her face and applying ointment to her *bruises, that were turning livid. Afterwards he brought her a sleeping potion, mixed in a cup of wine, and held it to her lips whilst she drank.*

He cried as he lay down beside her, whispering over and over how sorry he was for what he had done as he pressed into her hand a large emerald ring, mounted in gold.

It was six weeks before she recovered enough to leave his bed and he catered for her every need with a tenderness she knew could never last.

There had been many more degradations since then and many more of Marcellus's tortured tears, apologies and presents. None, however to match the splendour of the emerald ring that was now in the possession of the guard who would be on duty in the watchtower at the city gate that morning. It was a bribe for her and Daniel's freedom.

The birds had ceased their early morning chorus as she turned back to the window. The courtyard now stood empty and silent, yet still she waited. With a soft sigh of relief she saw the burly Syrian slave, who controlled Marcellus's household, returning from unlocking the gate in the outer wall, allowing for the delivery of fresh vegetables and fruit to the kitchen. As he passed beneath the window Marcellus stirred again and then settled more comfortably.

Cautiously she crossed the floor to the doorway where she paused to look back at him. Her eyes shifted to his dagger that lay unsheathed on the shelf above his head. She longed to reach for it but she knew that if she were to move close enough to threaten him, he would, as a trained soldier, sense her presence and her life would be over. Her body tensed for flight as she took one last look around before slipping silently from the room. As she disappeared, Marcellus opened his eyes, his lips twisting into an ugly sneer as he swung his legs over the side of the bed and sat up.

Chapter Two

Once outside the confines of the villa Leah made her way quickly to the wide colonnade that that ran from the west gate to the east, bisecting the city. Although still early people were already up and about their business and she slowed her pace, taking care not to attract attention. As she drew closer to the east gate her body began to tremble and her mouth dried. For a while she stood in the shadow of an upturned cart with a broken wheel; its load of barley grain spilled out across the ground. Her eyes narrowed as she looked up at the watchtower.

More carts, piled high with produce from the fields, were being trundled slowly through the gate. Carefully she adjusted her veil so that the lower part of her face was concealed and ducked between two carts that had come to a standstill. With a pounding heart she edged forward. Once on the other side of the wall she heaved a sigh of relief as she leaned against the rough stone, waiting for the strength to return to her limbs. Her hand trembled as she shaded her eyes and looked up again towards the watchtower. The guard had his back towards her.

For a moment she remained still, gathering her strength, before stumbling her way along the deeply rutted tracks to the valley below. Almost at the bottom she fell, scattering a shower of small stones that sent her sliding forward, grazing her hands and knees. As she regained her footing a sharp pain stabbed beneath her ribs, bending her double.

When it subsided she straightened and stood breathing deeply. With an effort of will she forced herself to run through a field of ripening wheat and on over the rough terrain for half a mile, until she reached a densely wooded area of tree and shrub. Almost spent of energy she arrived on the far side with a wildly beating heart, her breath coming in harsh gasps.

'Please let him be here, please let him be here,' she muttered. Relief flooded through her as Daniel emerged from out of the thicket leading two small grey horses.

He dropped the reins and ran towards her, rapidly covering the distance between them and wrapping his arms around her. She clung to him and she could feel the thumping of his heart. Gently she freed herself and moved back a step.

'I was afraid something might have happened to prevent you from coming.'

'Nothing could have stopped me,' he said, more sharply than he intended.

He frowned as his fingers gently stroked the scar that was standing out, livid on the pallor of her face.

'Hush now,' His voice had softened with tenderness and he hugged her to him again. 'It's going be all right. The guard let me out through the side gate with the horses an hour before dawn, as he promised.' He laughed without humour. 'When he sells that ring he will have more money than he ever dreamed of.'

'Did he ask you where we were going?'

He bit his lip and she held her breath.

'Yes, just as I was leaving. I told him we were going to Sychar.' Tears welled in his eyes. 'I should have said some other village.'

'Don't worry, Daniel. He won't betray us. It would mean him having to confess his part in our escape and give the ring back to Marcellus. He will not want to do that.'

He tried to smile, but failed, as he lifted her onto the smaller of the two animals.

'We need to get away. The trees are hiding us but we are too close to the city walls for comfort.'

The gold bangles around her wrist glinted in the sunlight, catching his eye, and she winced as his hand closed tightly around them.

'I know you didn't want to bring any of the jewellery that Marcellus gave you. But we need these bangles. Once they are sold we will have more than enough money to ensure our future.'

Abruptly he dropped her arm and turned to mount the other horse. His tunic was damp with perspiration and it clung to his skin as he sat loosely on the animal's back. He was just turned sixteen and she was suddenly conscious of how young and vulnerable he was. Desperately she regretted being persuaded into allowing him to arrange their escape. She knew Marcellus would not spare him if he caught up with them.

With the back of his hand Daniel wiped away the beads of sweat that had gathered on his top lip and picked up the reins.

'You did put a sleeping potion in Marcellus's wine last night?' he asked, the tremble in his voice betraying his nervousness.

'Yes, and he was snoring heavily when I left.'

'Then we will be well on our way to Sychar before he realises we are gone, and he will have no idea in which direction we have travelled.'

He managed a tight smile, with a look of bravery he was far from feeling, and she manoeuvred her horse closer to his, her voice quickening with fear.

'Listen to me Daniel. We have been careful. Marcellus has never discovered that you are my son and there's no reason why he should suspect you of helping me. I want you to go back before he realises you are missing. No one can handle that stallion of his as well as you. He trusts you with it. One day he will return to Rome and when that time comes he might reward you by making you a free man.'

Vehemently he shook his head. 'I'm not going back. You know as well as I, how unpredictable he is. He may do that, or sell me to another master. He may even kill me on a whim. Marcellus is capable of anything.'

The strain in his voice was palpable, and despite the increasing warmth of the early morning sun, she began to shiver.

'I'm so sorry, Daniel.'

He slipped from his horse and lifted her to the ground, stroking her hair that had tumbled loose, as her veil fell back. Winding a thick lock around his hand he bent his head and brushed it with his lips.

'We have come this far together, and we go on together. God delivered the people of Israel from bondage in Egypt and I have prayed to Him for our deliverance from Marcellus.'

As he spoke the boyish contours of his face took on the hard masculine lines of adulthood and she took a sharp intake of breath.

'When we planned this and you told me that you were Samaritan and not Jewish, as my father believed, I was shocked by your deceit. I still am.'

'Daniel, please, I...'

'No, let me finish. I know how much you want to see your sister Judith again, and that is why we are going to Sychar. But because of the religious differences, and the hostility that exists between Jews and Samaritans, I will have to hide the fact that my father was a Jew. That doesn't rest comfortably with me. I am proud of who I am and who he was. If she and her husband give us shelter I want you to remember your promise that our stay will only be for a short while. Then we go on to Jerusalem and make our home there because that is what my father would have wanted.'

She saw the fervour in his face and tears stung her eyes. 'I would never break a promise to you Daniel,' she said softly.

He hugged her to him and a hard note of determination entered his voice. 'We have both survived these past three years, each in our own way, and we will survive this. Now I make a promise to you. One day I will seek out those who sold us into slavery, after murdering my father and my grandmother, and I will avenge their deaths.'

He lifted her back onto her horse and remounted his own.

Chapter Three

Centurion Varinius stood leaning against the wall of the barn, the anxiety in his eyes giving lie to his relaxed appearance. Carefully he watched as Marcellus paced, vine stick in hand, impatient for the young groom to finish saddling the large grey stallion.

Small, and slight of build, the boy struggled to control the powerful beast that had sensed his tangible fear and was now pawing at the ground and snorting through dilated nostrils. Without warning Marcellus lunged forward and brought the stick down hard across the boy's back. As he reeled from the blow he lost his footing and crashed to the ground, his body curling into a ball to escape the flying hooves of the horse, as it reared and made a dash for the doorway.

In a blur of movement, and with the strength and reflexes honed in battle, Varinius caught the bridle and pulled hard, stalling the spooked animal in its bid for freedom. He led it back to the boy who was still lying on the ground, wide-eyed and terrified, blood streaking the back of his thin cotton tunic. For a moment he lay unmoving then he scrambled up and reached out for the horse with trembling hands. Once again the stallion reared, forcing him backwards. Marcellus laughed and it was an ugly sound. Ignoring him, Varinius walked slowly towards the boy and pulled him clear.

'Go! Get out,' he said, as he guided him, shivering towards the door. And then more gently, 'Have someone put an ointment on your back.'

He returned to the horse and with long firm strokes and soft words began to sooth the excited animal. When it calmed, he walked it to a stall at the rear of the barn and filled the manger with a bale of hay. As the horse began to eat he slowly backed away, closing the gate behind him. Then the two men faced each other. It was Marcellus who broke the uncomfortable silence.

'I see you still have the skill with horses that you learned in my father's stable,' he said. His eyes darted rapidly around, before fixing back on Varinius. 'It's been a long time since we last rode together.'

He tugged at the emerald ring on his little finger until it came loose and flung it across the floor to land at Varinius's feet.

'Take it, and make sure the guard gets it back, a reward for his help.' He gave a harsh, snort of breath. 'Leah and that boy were fools to think I wouldn't find out they had become lovers. They must have realised someone in my household would tell me they were together, laughing and talking, whenever I was away from home.'

His expression turned savage. 'I want to see their faces when I catch up with them. I'll have that boy tried by the magistrates as a runaway slave and for the theft of my horses. Then I'll take pleasure in forcing her to watch whilst he is crucified on a cross.'

Varinius shifted uneasily, disturbed by Marcellus's increasing instability. Without taking his eyes off him he bent to pick up the ring.

'I'm certain they are not lovers. And you told me you have already paid the guard well for his part in this. There's no need to give him the ring.'

'Keep it then, I don't want to see it again. And how can you be certain of anything? You only arrived at sundown yesterday, for the first time in months.'

Varinius gave a weary sigh. 'I want you to listen to me Marcellus. From all you told me last night your hand has been on this from the beginning. You could have stopped it at any time. But you chose to allow it to go on, so you could drag them back just when they thought they had gained their freedom. Your obsession with Leah is damaging you. For your own sake let her and the boy go.'

Marcellus rapped the vine stick against his leg and his face flushed.

'Who are you tell me what I should or shouldn't do? You seem to forget your mother was a servant in my father's house. It was only out of pity, after she was widowed, that he paid for you to be schooled with me. That education and his patronage are the only reasons you've been able to rise to the rank of centurion.' His voice turned mean and mocking. 'The truth is you don't want me to bring Leah back because you're jealous of her.'

He raised the vine stick, as though to strike, and moved a step closer. Varinius caught him by his arm and their eyes locked.

'I forget nothing. And I am not jealous of her. But mark this. Whatever my feelings for you, you will live to regret it if you use that stick.'

Roughly Marcellus wrenched himself free, spittle frothing at the corners of his mouth as he stumbled backwards.

'You have gone a step too far, centurion,' he screamed, as he struggled to regain his balance.

Varinius tilted his chin and watched him steadily for a moment before turning sharply and striding towards the doorway. Halfway there he stopped and looked back and there was an expression in his eyes that Marcellus had to turn from.

'Do you remember that day at the games in Rome, when we were boys, and you risked your life, dragging me from the path of a runaway horse and chariot?' he said softly. 'Well it is for the sake of that brotherhood we once had, and the debt of gratitude I owe your father, that I'm trying to help you now.'

The knuckles on the hand in which Marcellus held the vine stick stood out white from the tightness of his grip. Slowly he let it relax and the stick fell to the floor.

'Shall I tell you why I saved your life?'

'I know why,' Varinius said as he began walking back towards him.

'I don't think so. It was because if you had died I wouldn't have been able to bear seeing the pain in my father's eyes, screaming that it should have been me, not you.'

'Marcellus, don't...'

'Don't do what, tell the truth? We both know he sees in you the son he really wanted. He could hardly tolerate me near him after he beat my mother almost to death in front of me, before divorcing her for adultery, and forbidding her from ever seeing me again. I was six years old. No matter what I achieved after that it was never enough to win his love or approval, only his anger and demands that I do better.'

Varinius opened his mouth to speak and Marcellus held up a hand to stop him.

'I'm sorry for what I said. I know your rise from legionary to centurion has been on your own merit. And I've no doubt you will eventually be enrolled in the equestrian order, fulfilling all my father's ambitions for you.' He gave a bitter, half smile. 'It will make up for his disappointment in me. I have certainly failed to meet his aspirations and given him reason to despise me. But then he always has.'

'He doesn't despise you. You're his son. I was just his charity case.'

'You have never been a good liar, my friend. That haunted look in your eyes tells a different story.' His sigh was muted but the weight and the pain of it lay heavy between them.

'I loved your mother, Varinius, and I believe she loved me too. She was always there to comfort me after my father had beaten me or belittled something I had achieved. But never once did she look at me with that same proud smile with which she looked at you. I envied you that. I still do.'

As Varinius struggled to find words of comfort, Marcellus's mood shifted. Wiping the back of his hand roughly across his mouth, he began to pace once more, limping as he walked from the pain that had begun to throb in his hip. Coming to an abrupt halt he swung round.

'Let us consider for a moment this brotherhood between us, shall we? Because it hasn't been much in evidence of late. This is your first visit in months. Yet I know you travel between Jerusalem and Caesarea, quite frequently.'

'I stayed away because I don't like the company you keep, or what goes on in your home. It demeans you. But I have never stopped caring about you. And I am here now.'

Their eyes met and held and the silence was thick with tension until Marcellus cut through it, his voice rising shrill with rage.

'Don't stop now. I'm sure there's more you want to say. Let me hear it.'

Varinius's expression hardened. 'I was proud to serve under you as my tribune. But long before you were injured in battle your judgement had become suspect. You were drunk and unnecessarily brutal much of the time and your men lost respect for you. What went wrong?'

The outburst of rage he expected didn't come; instead Marcellus shrugged and his smile was sour.

'Nothing that hasn't always been wrong. But wasn't I lucky my injury provided the general with the excuse he needed to give me an honourable discharge. We both know I should have been disciplined and thrown out of the army in disgrace months sooner. And I would have been, but for his long-standing friendship with my father.'

Varinius failed to see him draw his sword until he felt the tip press into his neck. Then every sinew and muscle in his body tightened as he clasped the hilt of his own weapon. With a dry laugh Marcellus sheathed his sword again, his voice turning thick and guttural.

'Things turned out well for you though, didn't they? Promotion to senior centurion and a posting to Palestine. Was that arranged so you could keep an eye on me and report back to my father?'

With a swift intake of breath Varanius recoiled, as though from a physical blow. Marcellus slid to the floor with his back against the wall. Raising his knees he wrapped his arms around them.

'I shouldn't have said that. I know you would never act as a spy for him.'

'No, I would not,' Varinius said, a note of anger sharpening his tone. And your father had nothing to do with my posting here.' He dropped down on one knee and knelt in front of him. 'But I was glad to come because it meant I would see you again and be close if you needed me. Why did you leave Rome, after your discharge from the army?'

Marcellus shrugged. 'I couldn't bear the look of contempt in my father's face every time I met him. I'd inherited half my maternal grandfather's fortune, so I was no longer dependent on him. And I wasn't going to have him try to arrange some mediocre position for me, in the civil administration in Rome, in the hope I would eventually rise to a position of power.'

'Why Palestine?'

'It's as good a place as any. Sebaste is a thriving city. There are many opportunities for commercial ventures and I've increased my wealth considerably.'

There was defiant challenge in his voice that Varinius decided not to pursue. He stood and held out his hand.

'Get up. I am not going to stand by any longer watching you destroying yourself.'

Marcellus remained unmoving, his chin resting on his chest, his breathing shallow and laboured. 'I hate what I have become,' he whispered.

Losing patience Varinius hauled him from the floor and then placed a protective arm around his shoulders.

'For the sake of your health and sanity forget about Leah. You need rest now and to see a doctor.'

'I can't forget her. She consumes me.'

Anxious to get him home before anyone else arrived, Varinius began edging him towards the door. Before they were half way there Marcellus came to an abrupt halt and turned to face him, his mood shifting once more.

'There is nothing wrong with either my health or my sanity,' he said sharply. 'How long do you plan to stay?'

Varinius watched him steadily for a moment. 'Two days, three at most. The Zealots have been quiet for a while but that doesn't mean they're not plotting something. And there's a problem developing with the Jewish authorities. They are up in arms about a rabbi from Galilee, claiming he's perverting the Jewish people and rabble-rousing. But he poses no threat to Rome. He seems only to upset the religious sensitivities of the Jewish ruling classes with his preaching. The people in the countryside flock to hear…'

'The Zealots are dangerous in their desire to drive us out of Palestine,' Marcellus interrupted. 'But for all their scheming they will never be strong enough to make a successful rebellion against Rome. As for the priestly authorities, they must sort out their problems with this rabbi and do it quickly before it gets out of hand.'

Varinius remained thoughtful as though undecided about what he wanted to say. His voice when he spoke was cautious.

'I heard him preach a little while ago and I've talked with some of the sick he has cured. I've never met anyone like him, Marcellus. He's an extraordinary man. Perhaps when you are feeling better we could go together to listen to him.'

Marcellus's eyes widened in amazement. 'I have no intention of going anywhere to hear a Jewish rabbi preach, and especially not one from Galilee, who's stirring up trouble amongst his own people. I advise you to be very careful whom you associate with. Now, I'll saddle that horse and go after Leah and the boy. If I allow them to go free I'll be a laughing-stock.'

Varinius threw up his hands in resignation. 'All right! But you shouldn't be chasing after them yourself. Apart from anything else your hip won't stand the journey. Let me arrange for them to be brought back.'

A brief look of uncertainty crossed Marcellus's face, followed by a determined pursing of his lips.

'No! I shall go.'

'Then I go with you. They have had almost two hours start but those horses are old and slow. We should catch up with them before they reach Sychar.' His face was grave. 'But I want you to agree to bringing them back unharmed. And I want you to allow me to arrange their sale at the next slave auction, for your own good.'

The outburst of anger and argument he expected didn't come. Instead Marcellus nodded his head without meeting his eyes.

Chapter Four

Nestling on the lower slopes of Mount Ebal, overlooking the village at Sychar, the home that Tobiah had built for Rebekah stood illuminated in the hazy, golden glow of the late afternoon sun. Erected from rough-hewn stone, with a stairway at one end leading to a flat roof, it was considerably more generous in its proportions than those of his neighbours spreading out across the valley below.

Beyond the front of the house a narrow stony track meandered its way through an olive grove to the village before forking east for half a mile towards a flat plain and crossroads where the patriarch Jacob had dug his well. It was here the women from the village journeyed each morning to draw water and gossip.

In the courtyard pots of all shapes and sizes were neatly stacked beneath a canopy of woven palm leaves where Tobiah was sitting at his wheel. A tall slim man, not quite handsome but not plain either, there was about him the guarded reserve of a self-imposed loneliness that caused him to appear older than his twenty-four years.

As he revolved the wheel with his feet he moulded a deep-sided bowl with long tapering fingers, his face set into frown of concentration. Satisfied at last with its form he took up a small, sharp pointed tool and began incising a simple pattern into the soft, damp clay. As each section of the bowl was completed he examined it carefully for flaws with the expert eye of a craftsman. Finally content with its perfection, he set it aside to dry until it was ready for firing in the kiln.

To his relief a welcome westerly breeze, blowing in from the sea, had cooled the intense earlier heat of the day. His eyes felt tired and gritty and he rubbed them with his knuckles before standing up and stretching. Pushing his hands firmly into the small of his back he leant into them, easing the tension of several hours spent at his wheel. After one last, satisfied look at his collection of finished pots he strolled to the back of the house and stood watching the two donkeys grazing in a field patterned with the bright red of poppies.

A soft sigh escaped him as he turned to fill a bowl with rainwater that had collected in the large cistern. Bending down he removed his sandals and began to wash the dust from his feet. After drying them carefully he retraced his steps. As he entered his home a shiver ran through him and he paused on the edge of the dimly lit room.

A movement to his right attracted his attention and he turned, a rare smile lightening the soberness of his face as he looked down at the dog that had abandoned the bone it had been gnawing on to greet him. It was an odd-looking creature with startling yellow eyes and a long rough coat of black and grey hair. Its tail, mysteriously lost in a hillside adventure, was now a short tufted stump that was being wagged as furiously and proudly as though it were still its once splendid appendage.

With the whole length of its body quivering in excitement, the dog pushed and snuffled its long, pointed muzzle against his leg. He smiled with amused affection as he bent to run his hand down the back of the animal that had arrived at his door a year earlier, seven days after his wife Rebekah and their newborn son, who had lived for only two hours, had been buried. He had tended what remained of its sore and bleeding tail and they had remained inseparable ever since.

Rebekah was never far from his thoughts and he ached constantly, with an unrelenting grief, for the beautiful girl whose sense of mischief and fun had delighted his days. She had been his first love and they had been married for only a year when she had died. Since then his once joy filled world had become a lonely and desolate place. Desperately he clung to the bittersweet memory of her, fearful that time would erase her face and heal the pain that kept her image bright. With a gentle hand he pushed the dog away. Determined that the petting would continue the animal pawed at his leg with soft whimpers.

'Enough, enough,' he murmured. 'We will eat now and then walk down to the village and check on grandmother Ahava.'

He lifted a jug from the shelf that ran along a sidewall and filled a small bowl with water and another with a handful of grain and leftover pieces of dried goat's meat, setting them on the floor. For a while he watched as the dog greedily lapped up the water before devouring the food, and he envied its uncomplicated exuberance for life.

With little appetite he sat down to eat his own meal of corn porridge that had been prepared for him by Esther, the wife of Malachi, his farm steward. He ate slowly and without enjoyment, clearing his bowl before rising from the table to leave the house with the dog close at his heels. When they reached the olive grove the animal bounded forward in a headlong dash towards the village. Along the narrow streets the mud-brick houses crowded together around central courtyards that were alive with the noise of children playing and the voices of women, calling to each other as they cooked supper over charcoal and wood fires.

The home of Ahava stood alone, a little way off from the others, at the top of the village. She was sitting now outside her door on a rush mat in front of two circular millstones, where she had been grinding grain into flour for the next day's bread. Widowed and aging, her needs were few and simple, and she was well cared for. Even so, she suffered from that lonely disconnectedness that comes when the thrust and vigour of life has gone and responsibility has shifted to those younger and sharper. Bitterly she resented that she was no longer able make the long, daily journey to the well and enjoy gossiping there with the other women from the village. Instead she had learned to content herself with scolding their children, whenever they came within her reach, and sharing her unwanted wisdom with their mothers as they passed by, all the while pretending not to notice their polite, yet impatient, smiles.

Grinding the grain was an arduous task that needed two pairs of hands and Miriam, the daughter of Esther and Malachi, had been helping her. Now their work was done. It had been Miriam's job to gather the flour into piles as it flew out onto the skin beneath the stones and scoop them into small sacks. They had worked together in silence, the years that separated them too wide to bridge with idle talk, although Ahava's fondness for the girl was evident in the soft looks and smiles she gave her.

Sensing Tobiah's approach she lifted her head and beamed a wide, toothless smile. He lifted a hand in acknowledgement as he strode towards her, the dog running around him in ever widening circles and jumping high in the air in an effort to get him to throw the stick he was carrying. Miriam lowered her head and gave him a long sideways look from under her thick-fringe of lashes. It was a look that was not lost on Ahava.

'I think we have done enough for today. You can go home now, girl. Take the flour to your mother; she will need it for tomorrow's bread. Tell her from me you have worked well. I couldn't have managed without you.' She patted her arm.

Although glad to be released from the boredom of her task Miriam was now reluctant to leave. Gathering the sacks of flour she looked quickly up again at Tobiah as she rose gracefully from the mat. With a wave of her hand she skipped away on long slim legs. As Ahava watched her go, she waved in return, an affectionate smile lingering on her face. Then she shifted her gaze back to her grandson and took a deep breath.

'Miriam is such a sweet, obedient girl and a great help to me,' she said softly. 'She will soon be sixteen and Malachi and Esther must begin looking for a husband for her. Already they have left it very late.' She paused, the warning look in his eyes shutting off her words as he bent towards her and kissed her cheek.

'Leave it be, old woman.'

Although a gentle smile had softened what he said of any harshness she sought to repair the uncomfortable moment.

'Malachi has been telling me it will be a good harvest this year. The frequency of the late rains has been a blessing.'

'Mmm,' he murmured, avoiding her gaze as he lowered himself down beside her. 'I will be able to pay the Romans their taxes out of what we sell in the city, and there will be more than enough left over to see us and Malachi's family through the winter. When my pots are sold I'll be able to pay him a little more too.'

Ahava rested a hand, disfigured by dark spots and swollen knuckles, on top of his.

'That will be welcome. He and Esther need all the money they can get if they are to provide a good dowry for Miriam. Your grandfather would have been proud of you, Tobiah. You have managed the farm well.'

As the silence lengthened uncomfortably between them he lowered his head and began stroking the dog that had settled by his side. When he looked up again his eyes were guarded and his face unsmiling.

'I don't care about the land like he did,' he said, his voice harsh. Seeing the sadness in her face he felt a flush of shame and tenderly stroked her cheek. 'It's Malachi we have to thank for the way the farm has prospered. He was a loyal steward to my grandfather and he is honest and loyal to me. Without him I could never find the time to do what I like best: working at my father's craft of pottery.'

Relieved by his gentler tone, she nodded. 'You couldn't have a better steward than Malachi and Esther looks after me like a daughter. I'm glad you leased those five acres to their sons at a price they could afford. Being able to grow crops on their own patch will make a tremendous difference to their lives.'

Tobiah's laugh was tinged with envy. 'I know, particularly as there always seems to be another baby coming along to one or the other of them.'

'Malachi and Esther are truly blessed in their family,' Ahava said softly. 'And Miriam is so beautiful and such a good child she is sure to marry well.' She tried to smile but a heavy weight of sadness stung her eyes with tears.

Unwilling to be drawn into any further conversation about the virtues of Miriam, Tobiah, sought to distract her.' I'm not happy about you being here alone, grandmother. When grandfather died so soon after Rebekah and I were married, you should have come to live in my home then. Come now, it will make it easier for Esther and Miriam to care for us.'

She shook her head. 'I know you think I'm a stubborn old woman. But this is the home that Joseph's grandfather built, and where Joseph brought me as a bride. It is where my children were born and it is where I want to die.'

Tobiah knew, from long experience, the futility of trying to plead with her to change her mind once it was made up, and they fell into the restful silence of two people comfortably at ease with each other.

Slowly Ahava's thoughts drifted back to that hot summer day when Tobiah had been ten years old, and plague was once again ravaging the country. The last time it visited it had been her nineteen-year-old son, Reuben, it had claimed. This time it was her daughter, Judith, and her husband Thomas. They had died within two hours of each other, leaving Tobiah orphaned.

In the afternoon following their burial she had found him lifting out one the several clay pots still in his father's kiln. As she replayed the scene in her mind she could see and hear the two of them as clearly as though it were happening now.

She approached him with a soft tread, so that he wouldn't be startled, but still he heard her coming. Silently he lifted his head and watched her draw close, his small face pinched and grey as he handed her the pot he was holding. His eyes, luminous with unshed tears, never left her face as she took it in her hands. She smiled at him and turned the pot around, carefully appraising it.

'It's very good, Tobiah. Your father was the best potter in the whole of Samaria. One day, you too will make fine pottery, just like he did. Your grandfather will help you practise on his wheel and he will dig and clean the clay for you and fire the kiln, until you are big and strong enough to do it for yourself.'

He heaved a long sigh. Putting down the pot she held out her arms and gathered him up, folding him to her breast. Tenderly she stroked the top of his head as she smiled down on him. His grip tightened around her as though he would never let her go. Then he pulled away from the circle of her arms and stood looking at her, wary and anxious, his words coming out in a rush.

'Sometimes, I think my grandfather doesn't like me very much. He always seems uncomfortable when I am near him. And he never wants me in the fields with him. I don't think he will be happy to have me live with you.'

Her heart thumped uncomfortably fast in her chest and her voice was sharper than she intended.

'What foolishness, Tobiah. Of course your grandfather loves you and wants you to live with us.'

She took him in her arms once more and held him close.

With a deep shudder she became aware again of her surroundings and that her face was wet with tears. Without warning, long suppressed memories that she had believed buried forever began crowding in, and she clenched her fists. She breathed hard and her nostrils dilated as she struggled to fight down the painful image of another child, broken and terrified. Her beautiful, tawny-gold eyes were filled with tears and staring accusingly into hers.

As though from a distance she heard Tobiah calling her name as he bent over her, his hand pressing into her shoulder.

'Grandmother, are you all right,' he kept repeating, his voice edged with fear.

'Yes, of course I am, Tobiah' She struggled to sit up straight as she wiped away her tears with the palms of her hands.

Unconvinced, he shook his head. 'You look pale and you are crying. I'll go to Malachi's house and get Esther.'

Drawing on strength she didn't know she had she smiled and squeezed his hand in reassurance.

'No, that's not necessary. Truly, I am all right now.' Her voice tripped. 'I was just re-visiting the past and thinking about how much I miss your mother.' She turned her head, unable to look at him in case he saw the deception in her eyes.

'I miss her too, grandmother, and I miss my father,' he said, as he sat down again by her side.

She patted his shoulder and he felt a surge of relief as he saw the colour beginning to return to her face.

'I sent word to Matthias last month that I shall be taking my pots to Sebaste tomorrow, to sell in his shop. Is there anything I can bring you back? What about some bangles or necklaces, eh! Or a silk shawl?' he joked, attempting to lighten the atmosphere between them.

Her heartbeat had returned to its normal rhythm and she managed a smile as she gently scolded him with a sly sideways look.

'I can do without trinkets from city shops, and silk shawls that we can't afford. What a waste of money they would be if I don't live until you get back,'

Grateful for the lifting of her mood Tobiah laughed. 'You, old woman, will have to live forever because you would cause too much trouble in heaven,' he teased.

She gave him her fiercest frown. Hiding a smile behind one hand, she fumbled in the bowl beside her with the other, seeking a fig to throw to the dog. It snatched at it, swallowing it in an instant, then inched forward until its wet nose was pressing against her side, its eyes begging for more. Getting up from the mat Tobiah stood in front of her and placed a hand on her head in a tender benediction, a dread rising in his breast as he realised how thin and fragile she had become.

'Are you sure you will be all right, whilst I'm gone? Is there anything you need?'

She shook her head. 'Esther will be here soon with my supper and to help me to bed and Miriam will bring me fresh water from the well tomorrow. No one could be better looked after. All I need is for you to come home safely.'

'Don't worry about my safety.' He nodded towards the dog. 'I have a good protector.' His smile didn't quite reach his eyes. 'And you don't need to remind me that Matthias's wife was the sister of Rebekah and that this will be my first visit since I buried her and our son.'

A strained silence settled between them and a deep fear clutched at her as she recognised her own frailty. It wasn't the inevitability of her death that frightened her; in many ways she would welcome it. It was leaving him alone that tore at her heart.

'I'm ashamed, grandmother,' he said, so softly she had to lean forward to hear him. 'Matthias has been my friend since we were boys, when he lived in the village. Now I am envious of him. It will be hard to hold his first born in my arms and eat supper with him and Martha and see their contentment.'

She took his hand in hers and turned it over to kiss his palm. 'If I could remove the ache from your heart and bear it myself, Tobiah, I would. But it won't remain this way forever. In time you will find peace, and then the once happy memories that cause you such sorrow now will become sweet again. Go with my blessing and come back safely.'

For a heartbeat they remained unmoving and then she released his hand. Calling the dog to his side, he set off towards his home. The dying rays of the setting sun were burnishing the sky with a fiery glow as he turned to give her a final farewell wave. She lifted her hand in return and watched him as he stooped to pick up a stick and throw it in a wide arc for the excited dog to chase.

'May the God of our father Abraham help you find a good wife soon, Tobiah, so I can die in peace. One who will bring you comfort and bear you many strong sons. You can't grieve forever,' she whispered.

He paused and looked back, almost as though he had heard, and the sadness in his eyes brought a welling of tears to hers.

On the following morning, an hour before daybreak, he was in the field at the back of his house, loading the pots that were ready for sale into his cart. The donkey, with head drooping, stood waiting patiently for the journey to begin. Although the sky was clear and star filled, and the moon bright, he lit a lamp to help guide his way until the sun rose. The heavy dew had soaked his feet and sandals, causing him to shiver in the cool air, and he wrapped his cloak around him.

His journey across the plains and valleys would take almost three hours before he finally reached the bustling, cosmopolitan city of Sebaste.

Chapter Five

Tobiah arrived at the city gate dusty, weary, and thankful to have come safely to the end of his long journey as Marcellus and Varinius were galloping through. Their horses clipped the side of his cart causing it to rock dangerously, spilling out two of his pots that smashed as they hit the ground. Braying and quivering in terror the donkey kicked out its back legs endangering the cart and its contents even further as Tobiah struggled to calm him.

Marcellus turned in his saddle and shook his fist, whilst mouthing an obscenity. Sure-footed and fleet, the horses raced down the hillside, scattering stones beneath the beat of their hooves. Always the better rider of the two, Marcellus led the way. Looking back over his shoulder, he grinned at Varinius who raised a hand in salute whilst urging his horse on to draw level. Despite his misgivings he couldn't help but rejoice in the unexpected thrill and camaraderie of riding with Marcellus once more.

For an hour they raced across the hilly terrain before dropping into a long, wide valley. Varinius slowed and Marcellus waved an arm, calling to him to keep up the pace.

'We should catch sight of them soon,' he yelled.

Laughing, he broke into song and Varinius joined in. As he pounded ahead he took the lead, forcing Marcellus to spur on his horse until they were again neck and neck, the drumming of hooves almost drowning out the sound of their singing. For a while, they rode in silence until Marcellus, who was once again in front, held up his hand and reined in his horse, allowing Varinius to draw alongside him.

'See, there, just beyond that outcrop to the left where the path begins to climb.'

Varinius strained forward. Raising his hand to shield his eyes against the glare of the sun he peered into the distance.

'Yes, I see them. They are walking to rest the horses.'

Marcellus pointed a finger. 'Look, if we take that track to the right and skirt around the vineyard we can cut them off as they climb out of the valley.'

Varinius frowned. 'Before we go any further I want you to remember your promise. We take them back unharmed,' he said sharply.

Marcellus nodded in acknowledgment and spurred his mount forward.

As Leah, Daniel and the two small horses struggled up the last steep incline and onto the wide, stony road and open plain, they found their way barred by the two men.

Heedless for her own safety, Leah stepped in front of Daniel, shielding him with her body. Marcellus dismounted and walked towards them, his limp more pronounced because of the acuteness of the pain in his hip, caused by the long ride over rough terrain. He stopped within arms reach of her.

Varinius remained astride his horse, holding the reigns loosely in one hand and letting the other rest on the hilt of his sword, his eyes trained on the back of Marcellus.

In the dry, hot stillness time seemed to dissolve, as they stood fixed in a bizarre tableau. An eagle, drifting high above them on the warm air currents rising from the valley, was the only movement.

Daniel's eyes were wide with fear and his face had paled. Slowly he began edging around to Leah's side. She took hold of his hand and gripped it hard and he struggled to control the trembling of his limbs as they both stared at Marcellus.

He was blinking rapidly as he looked from one to the other of them. Then he settled on Daniel. Never before had he looked properly at the boy. The sharp taste of bile rose in his throat. His eyes were Leah's eyes, beautiful, mesmerising and darkening now with fear from tawny-gold to brown. He felt the heavy beat of a pulse start up in his temple and his lips stretched across his teeth in a rictus grin.

'So, Leah, I see it now. I thought you had developed a passion for young boys and taken him as your lover, but he's your son. That's why, when I bought you, you begged me to buy him too.'

He gasped and bent forward, struggling through a sudden onslaught of pain that was gripping his chest like a vice. His hand fell towards the hilt of his sword and despite his pain there was a malevolent menace in his look.

'Now why have I never noticed the likeness before?'

Frantically Leah flung herself to the ground at his feet and grabbed at the hem of his cloak.

'I beg you, Marcellus, don't hurt him. He's just a boy. I made him help me. I'll come back with you. I'll do anything you want.' Her voice rose shrill with fear. 'Only please, don't hurt him.'

'He means that much to you, does he, Leah?'

With mounting panic she realised that she had made a terrible mistake in pleading so passionately for Daniel.

Breathing heavily he stared down at her. The pain in his chest eased and he lunged forward. Roughly he grabbed her arm, his fingers biting into her flesh as he dragged her up, almost lifting her off her feet. With a roar Daniel leapt towards him. In an instant Marcellus had released his hold on her and drawn his sword. The blade flashed in the sun. Steadying himself he drove the point into Daniel's chest. As he withdrew his weapon Daniel fell backwards, his limbs twisting, his eyes wide open with a look of shocked surprise.

For a moment there was utter silence then, with a high-pitched wail, Leah scrambled to her feet. With her hands outstretched she flung herself at Marcellus, reaching for his face. Taking a stumbling step sideways he knocked her to the ground where her head hit against a rock as she fell. Unsteadily he raised his sword to strike again. Varinius, who had dismounted, ran towards him, seizing him around his shoulders.

'No!' he yelled, tightening his hold as Marcellus struggled to break free.

With strength born of rage and madness he thrust Varinius aside and swung round towards Leah who had crawled across to Daniel. Half sitting, half lying, she was cradling his body and closing his eyes that had been staring up at her, glazed and empty.

'Kill me too, Marcellus,' she said, her voice a ragged whisper. 'You have taken from me the only person who made my life bearable.'

Like a man drunk on too much wine he swayed and clutched at his chest as the pain gripped him again. He opened his mouth to speak but no words came and his sword dropped from his hand. Varinius caught him as he fell, reeling under his weight as he struggled to keep his balance and lay him down.

Rocking Daniel to her breast, Leah watched as he knelt beside Marcellus' lifeless body. Tenderly he lifted him into his arms, his face masked by an anguish that matched hers for her son. With a sob catching in her throat, she carefully rested Daniel on the ground and dragged herself towards him until she was close enough to clutch at his foot.

'Please, finish it. He wanted me dead. I beg you, end it now.' Her voice faded as he lifted his head and looked at her.

Gently he laid Marcellus down and stood with his back to the sun, his shadow falling across her. She watched as his hand moved to the hilt of his sword and she closed her eyes, welcoming the blow that would end her pain.

'Look at me,' he said. And although he spoke without raising his voice, it was command not a request.

Her head throbbed. As she struggled to force open her eyes she heard him give a lingering sigh.

'I will not kill you, Leah. You must live with your grief for Daniel, as I must live with mine for Marcellus. I will bury your son. Then I will take Marcellus back to the Sebaste where I will make sure he has the funeral of an honourable Roman. No one will know what happened here today. If anyone asks, I shall say Marcellus collapsed and died before we caught up with you.'

With ease he lifted Daniel's lifeless body in his arms and carried him beyond the road. Stopping beneath the gnarled branches of an ancient oak tree he set him down. Purposefully he began to scratch out a shallow grave with his dagger. When it was done he laid Daniel in and covered his body with the dry, dusty earth and a mound of small stones.

Leah remained unmoving on the ground, her hair matting with the blood that was seeping from the wound on her head. With long determined strides he strode back towards her. As she watched him, through half closed eyes, his body appeared to dissolve and reappear, phantom like, in the shimmering heat haze.

For a while he stood looking down on her, as though undecided. Then he dropped onto one knee and took the emerald ring from his tunic, putting it into her hand and closing her fist around it. As though she were no weight at all he picked her up and carried her to Daniel's grave. Laying her down he covered her with his cloak and placed his water skin by her side. Then took a step back. She closed her eyes but she could feel him standing there, looking down at her.

'I am sorry,' he said, in a voice surprisingly tender. When you have recovered try and continue on your journey to Sychar.'

Without looking back he walked to where the horses she and Daniel had been riding were grazing. Quickly he removed their bridles and drove them off. With barely a struggle he lifted the dead weight of Marcellus's body across the back of his stallion and secured him with the bridles. After one last look around the open plain he mounted up, gathering the reigns with one hand and reaching for Marcellus's horse with the other. Leah pulled his cloak over her head and closed her eyes.

Chapter Six

After Marcellus and Varinius had disappeared in a storm of dust Tobiah began to calm his donkey and quieten the frantically barking dog. The noisy commotion had drawn the attention of one of the city watchmen, a man who had once lived in Sychar, and who his grandfather had often hired to work on the farm at harvest time. As he came to help gather up the pieces of broken clay Tobiah smiled at him.

'It seems someone is in a great hurry this morning,' he said.

The man smiled back, although his eyes were wary. Then he shrugged his shoulders and leaned closer.

'Yes, and from the look on their faces I wouldn't like to be on the receiving end of their visit.'

With a frown Tobiah gave a nod of agreement. The watchman placed a hand to the side of his mouth as though about to say something more, then he changed his mind.

'Make haste to pick up those pieces and then get on about your business,' he ordered briskly.

Slowly and deliberately Tobiah kicked the remaining bits of broken clay to one side and called to the dog, lying panting and watchful by the side of the cart. Taking up the reigns of the donkey, he urged it forward through the gates. The reek of livestock that had been brought in earlier by the drovers, and the strong smell of the leather being sold by the tanners, assailed his nostrils as he passed.

Walking without haste he crossed the square and turned right, entering the maze of narrow streets and alleyways. When he reached Matthias's shop he was standing in his doorway seeing out a customer who had bought a large water jar. A broad smile lit up his face as he saw Tobiah and he held his arms out wide as he rushed to greet him, kissing him on both cheeks.

'Welcome, Tobiah. It is good to see you again. Come, I have wine ready to revive you and then we will unload your pots. As you can see, the streets are already busy.'

He draped an arm around his friend's shoulders as he ushered him into the dim interior of his shop, where pots of all shapes and sizes crowded the shelves and floor. A small smile of satisfaction pulled at the corners of Tobiah's lips as he noticed the space that had been left empty, waiting for his.

With a sigh of relief that his journey was over he sat on a stool, whilst Matthias poured water into a bowl for him to wash his hands and the thick dust from his feet. After throwing him a towel, he began busily uncorking a wine jar. Carefully he measured the liquid into two cups and passed one to Tobiah before filling a small bowl with water for the dog. It lapped noisily until sated. With dripping muzzle, the animal flopped to the ground beside Tobiah, its head resting between its two front paws.

Matthias looked from him to the dog and laughed, his eyes dancing with delight at being in the company of his friend once more. Putting his wine cup carefully onto a small table he lowered himself down, to sit cross-legged on a rush mat, and held out his hands.

'Now, tell me all your news. How is grandmother Ahava?'

Tobiah took a mouthful of his wine, savouring it slowly. 'She's looking frail, and every one of her years. I worry about her. However, she is as spirited as ever and sends her blessings to you and your family.'

He tilted back his head and his mouth twisted into a smile that didn't reach his eyes. 'I think she wants to marry me off to Miriam, Malachi's daughter.'

Matthias looked at his friend with a sad intensity as he cleared his throat and rose from the mat. Nervously he shifted his weight from one foot to the other.

'Perhaps it is time to think of marrying again, Tobiah. You could do far worse than the daughter of a man who has been a like a father to you. Miriam is young and strong; she would bring comfort to your home and perhaps bear you many sons.'

He paused, surprised and embarrassed by the fervour of his speech. 'Rebekah wouldn't want you to remain alone,' he said, clasping his hands tightly in front of him.

Without answering, Tobiah drained his wine cup and clicked his fingers. The dog sat up and placed a large paw on his knee and he ran his hand down its back, smoothing the thick hair that instantly sprang up again, and then he too stood.

'Let us unload my cart, Matthias, and afterwards you can tell me about this new son of yours and how Martha is enjoying being a mother.'

Left feeling uncomfortable by Tobiah's lack of response to what he had said, Matthias smiled nervously. 'They are both well, as you will see for yourself later.'

In an attempt to mend the awkwardness between them, he placed an arm around Tobiah's shoulders.

'We both love you, Tobiah, and want to hear you laugh again and be happy. Martha is longing to see you. She hopes you can both take comfort from your shared memories of Rebekah.'

Tobiah took a sharp intake breath and then he had to look away, for fear of betraying the rage that had filled him since the death of his wife and son.

'I can't talk about her because every memory I have only makes her loss more bitter and the lonely emptiness more painful,' he said abruptly.

Helplessly Matthias shook his head, not knowing what to say to breach the gulf that had opened up between them. The arrival of customers broke the tension and Matthias bustled to serve them.

As the morning wore on the streets became crammed with people and the clatter of chariots and carts. Neighbours met and gossiped and shopkeepers and vendors shouted in praise of their wears, with good-natured rivalry, all adding to the rising cacophony of noise.

Towards noon, as the heat of the day intensified, the enticing aromas of cooking food rose and lingered in the air, mingling with the smell of sweat from the crowds. As the streets began to quieten Matthias closed his shop and they went out to find somewhere to eat.

It was late afternoon when they opened up again and once more the streets began to throng. An hour before sundown many pots had been sold including, to Tobiah's satisfaction, most of his. The money belt around his waist felt gratifyingly heavy. Slowly the clamour began to subside as people hurried to return to their homes before the dangers of nightfall.

Matthias went outside to pull the wooden grill across the front of the shop, calling for Tobiah to come and help. He nodded as he replaced the pot he had been examining back on its shelf. As he walked towards the door the dog appeared from behind a large urn where it had been sleeping. Placing its front paws squarely on the ground it raised its hindquarters and stretched its back, before ambling to Tobiah's side.

Matthias threw back his head and laughed. 'I swear that animal is never going to let you out of its sight. Come on, let's finish closing up then we can go home. Martha will have supper ready and you can, at last, meet my son.'

They left the shop with Tobiah leading the donkey and the dog trotting close by his side. Puffs of rising dust blackened their sandaled feet and the hem of their tunics as they walked. They talked easily together, with the comfortable familiarity of old friends, as they wound their way through the narrow cobbled streets.

As the commercial quarters gave way to a small, paved square they were hailed by a group of men standing beside a fountain, exchanging gossip about the day's business. Adam, the little man who sold bread and cakes from a counter at the front of his bakery, detached himself from the group and made his way towards them, his face wreathed in smiles. He enclosed Tobiah in a pair of surprisingly strong arms and stood on tiptoe to kiss his cheeks. His gentle brown eyes clouded with sadness as he released him and stood back.

'It's good to see you again Tobiah. It has been a long time, but you have been in my thoughts. I am sorry for your loss.'

Tobiah nodded and turned his head without answering. Adam shuffled his feet uneasily. Seeking to ease his embarrassment, Matthias smiled broadly and clapped him on his back.

'Come, Adam, tells us the days news. There is no gossip passes you by,' he said, with an affectionate laugh.

Tobiah had the grace to look ashamed as Adam glanced nervously at him. He was uncertain of his ground but suddenly he bristled with excitement at the chance to tell the news.

'Well!' He paused, enjoying the suspense. 'I heard that one of the wealthy Romans of our city rode out with a centurion this morning and came back dead across his saddle.'

Tobiah nodded. 'I saw them leaving as I arrived. They were in a great hurry. In fact they almost demolished my cart.'

A thoughtful silence settled between them until Matthias shrugged his shoulders.

'Good riddance! One less Roman in our country,' he said dryly.

Tobiah raised a hand in warning and Matthias tilted his chin in defiance.

For a while longer they remained in conversation before taking their leave of Adam and continuing on their homeward journey. The smell of baking bread, drifting towards them from the many outdoor ovens, began to sharpen their hunger and as they drew closer to Matthias's home they quickened their pace. It wasn't long before they arrived.

Matthias hurried inside whilst Tobiah busied himself tying his donkey to a post, and tipping out a bag of hay. As he stepped across the threshold he heard Matthias calling out for Martha. She emerged from out of the shadows and moved into a pool of lamplight, cradling the child and smiling shyly. Beaming, Matthias beckoned him forward.

'Tobiah, meet my son,' he said, with unconcealed pride.

For a heartbeat Tobiah hesitated then he stepped further into the room and moved towards Martha. Gently he took the child from her and held him in one arm, close to his breast. He lifted back the shawl that covered him and looked down into the small sweet face, giving a gasp of shock when he saw how much he resembled Rebekah. With soft, mewling sounds the baby waved his hands in the air. As he found his mouth he began sucking noisily on his fist, gazing up at Tobiah through wide innocent eyes.

Matthias and Martha held their breath and tightly gripped hands. When Tobiah looked up at them the harsh lines and soberness of his face was transfigured by a smile that finally reached his eyes, and he held the child closer.

'Look, Martha, see how much he resembles Rebekah. He has her mouth and her eyes. And yes, I'm sure that he has her nose too. See how she lives on in him.'

His voice broke and the tears, so long denied, spilled down his cheeks as something inside him began to stir and come alive.

'How beautiful he is, how Rebekah would have loved him. If our son had lived they would have been as close as brothers.'

Martha moved to his side and wrapped her arms around both him and the baby. Then she turned to pull Matthias towards them. They stood, the three of them, grouped together, grinning foolishly, each reluctant to break the spell of hope and new beginnings that the child was weaving.

It was the ever-practical Matthias who was the first to move. With a broad smile he bustled about, filling two bowls with water so they could wash the dust from their feet. Martha carefully took the baby from Tobiah's arms and returned him to his crib.

Over supper, Matthias, always more garrulous than his friend, entertained them with tales of what went on in the city, waving his hands in the air excitedly as he talked. Through half closed eyes, Tobiah watched Martha and tried to stifle his rising feeling of envy at the look of love and admiration on her face as she listened to her husband.

When supper was over, and Matthias and Martha had retired with their son, he picked up the rolled mattress she had left for him and strolled out into the courtyard that was lying silvered in moonlight. For the first time since Rebekah had died he felt at peace. As he climbed the stairs to the roof of the house a cloud, drifting on the breeze, blotted out the light. He stood, motionless in the shadows, his head thrown back as he pondered on what had happened as he held the child. Quicksilver emotions that now evaded his grasp but which he knew, with a deep certainty, he would capture again. He unrolled the mattress and lay down, covering himself with his cloak.

At sunrise the following morning he was ready to leave as Matthias appeared, sleepily running his fingers through his hair. He held out his arms and Tobiah moved towards him.

'My friend, I must set off for home. I am anxious to get back to my grandmother. And Malachi will be fretting about the barley harvest and wanting to hire the labourers and get it underway.'

Matthias nodded. 'I know, its a busy time. I just wish you could be with us for longer. When the rest of your pots sell I'll keep the money safe for you. Don't let too much time go by before we see you again.' he said anxiously.

With a warm smile crinkling the corners of his eyes Tobiah put a hand on his shoulder.

'Don't worry. I won't let anything keep me from watching your son grow and being a part of his life. Tell Martha motherhood suits her. She is more beautiful than ever.'

Matthias grinned. 'I will not tell her that, She has become far too sure of herself of late. There will be no controlling her if she gets any worse.'

Tobiah laughed softly at this inconceivable image of the shy, gentle Martha, and cuffed him on his head. Then there was a sudden, awkward silence between them. Each was feeling reluctant to take his leave of the other, and both were acutely conscious of the many things left unsaid that were still too new and delicate to be bruised by words.

Matthias opened his arms and held Tobiah for a long moment, then released him and bent to pick up the bag he had place on the ground.

'Here take this for your journey,' he said, brushing the tears from his cheeks. 'Martha has put a loaf and some cheese in, and she has filled your water skin too. Go with care, my friend.'

Anxious now to be on his way Tobiah gave him another hug and then quickly strapped his donkey into the shafts of the cart. With an amused smile he raised an eyebrow as the dog jumped aboard and stood on its hind legs, its front paws resting over the side, eyes alert for any movement at which it could bark a warning. As he urged the donkey forward he gave a last farewell wave to Matthias standing framed in the doorway.

Chapter Seven

The streets were already beginning to bustle as Tobiah made his way towards the city gate. The watchman who had helped him pick up the pieces of broken pots the previous day, saw him and held up an arm, bringing him to a halt. Leaping from the cart the dog bounded to Tobiah's side and crouched low, a warning growl rumbling deep in its throat. The man's face creased with good-natured amusement.

'As long as you've got that animal you can travel anywhere in safety. No one would dare come near you,' he said.

Tobiah laughed as the dog stretched out quietly, its nose resting on its front paws in feigned submission, ears twitching at every movement.

'Yes, I know. It would be a brave man who would attempt to rob me.'

'Well, I certainly wouldn't. Pull over a bit. There are three carts coming in piled high with grain. You can go through as soon as they've passed.'

With a nod Tobiah guided his donkey to the side of the wall whilst the watchman, in talkative mood, followed.

'I expect the gossip reached the streets yesterday?'

Tobiah shifted uneasily. 'I didn't have the time for listening to gossip, I was kept busy selling my pots.'

'Ah, so there were rumours then.' The man's eyes gleamed knowingly and he tilted his head to one side.

'There are always rumours in this city and often they amount to nothing,' Tobiah replied, with a shrug of his shoulders.

Lowering his voice to a whisper, the watchman leant towards him. 'This time they do. Do you remember yesterday, when the centurion and his friend nearly demolished your cart in their mad dash through the gates as you arrived?'

He watched him, savouring the moment, his eyes glittering in anticipation of Tobiah's reaction. When he remained silent he hurried on, determined to create an interest.

'When they came back the centurion was leading the horse belonging to the other one, who was face down across the saddle, Dead, the life snuffed out of him,' he said triumphantly.

Tobiah shrugged his shoulders. 'Other than the taxes I have to pay, Rome and her citizens are none of my business.'

Much disgruntled by Tobiah's lack of interest, he drew himself up.

'The gate is clear now. You can go on your way. Remember me to your grandmother. She was kind to me as a boy and your grandfather always found me work on his farm at harvest time.'

With deliberately unhurried steps, Tobiah led the donkey forward, calling to the dog as he went. The animal pricked up his ears and bounded forward, jumping aboard the cart as it trundled through the gate. Once outside he brought the donkey to a halt and looked out across the countryside towards Mount Gerizim, the sacred mountain where his people worshipped God. A surge of well being swept through him and he closed his eyes to offer up a prayer of thanks for the happiness he had known with Rebekah, and for the blessing of this unforeseen peace in her memory.

From the moment he had held his friend's son in his arms and looked into his small face, which so resembled hers, he had felt her spirit leading him from despair to a place where new beginnings were possible. She had filled his life with love and joy and left her imprint on his soul. Now he dared to believe he might find happiness once more.

A soft smile played at the corners of his mouth as he thought of his grandmother's ill-concealed desire for him to marry Miriam, and the pleasure that it would bring her. With a sense of release, he realised that the feeling of betrayal that had held him back was no longer overshadowing the possibility of their union and the sons she might bear him. Still smiling, he led the donkey forward, the sturdy little animal placing its feet carefully as the cart rocked from side to side as they began their descent.

As the morning wore on and the heat from the sun intensified, he shed his cloak, letting it rest over the side of the cart where the dog lay panting, its long, pink tongue lolling out to one side. Gradually he became conscious of the strengthening wind and the countryside around him as the valley shelved onto the wide plain.

On the eastern horizon the mountaintops had become shrouded in cloud and the wide ribbon of sky, visible in the gap between them, had darkened to deep purple. He frowned, concerned that the crops might be damaged. The rains should have ceased by now he thought. In a sudden flurry of movement the dog jumped from the cart, its ears flattening. Raising its head to the sky it began to howl at the quickening storm clouds that were rolling above.

Quickly Tobiah snatched up his cloak, and wrapped it around him, as large drops of rain spattered on the ground and then began falling in a fast torrent. The stony dirt road soon became a river of mud as lightning streaked the sky and thunder rumbled. He moved to stand by the donkey's head. His sodden cloak and tunic were clinging to his body and water dripped from his beard and hair as he sought to calm the frightened animal.

The dog gave one last howl at the sky and shook its body, water flying off in a shower of glistening drops as it bounded across the open plain. Tobiah yelled after it to return but the animal paid no heed.

Almost as suddenly has it had begun the storm subsided, and the sun burned bright again. Tobiah removed his cloak and carefully spread it across a bush to dry.

Deftly he unhitched the sodden and forlorn looking donkey from the cart that was awash, and tipped it up, allowing the water to run out. After backing the donkey into the shafts again, he raised a hand to shade his eyes and looked to where the dog was pawing around a tree. He called and the animal lifted its head, barking twice before resuming foraging. Impatiently he made his way towards it, shouting commands that went unheeded.

As he drew nearer the dog looked up and ran to him, tugging at the hem of his tunic and pulling him forward. He pushed it off and went down on one knee to look closer. Cautiously he began removing the debris from a bundle of sodden material. He stopped, hand in mid air, as he heard a muffled moan coming from beneath what he now recognised to be the cloak of a Roman officer. In panic he scrambled to his feet, grabbing the dog by its scruff, as he looked frantically around. The only sign of life was a camel train on the horizon, slowly winding its way along one of the eastern trade routes, towards the coastal road.

With curiosity overcoming his fear, he let go of the dog and reached out a trembling hand. Cautiously he pulled back a corner of the cloak, his eyes widening in horror as he stared down into the face of a barely conscious woman. Her hair was matted with blood and the fist of her right hand lay tightly clenched across her breast, as though concealing something. Slowly he backed away, his breath coming in short rasping gasps. He turned and broke into a run, calling for the dog to follow him, and then he stopped and looked back. The animal was still where he had left it, its feet planted firmly and its hindquarters raised as it tugged at the Roman cloak.

Against his better judgement, and with a fast beating heart, he made his way back to the tree. Briefly he hesitated, unsure, then he pushed the dog away and lifted the woman into his arms and she moaned in protest. Fear rose in his breast like a thick black tide when he saw that she had been lying across a makeshift grave, from which a foot protruded.

He held her easily, despite her feeble attempts to break free, and raced back to the cart. He gasped for breath as he heaved her in, laying her awkwardly in the small space, her head resting against the side. With trembling hands he made a pillow of his still damp cloak, his fingers fumbling as he pushed it behind her head. Carefully he placed his water skin to her lips, telling her to drink. She moaned in protest and feebly tried to push him away before allowing the liquid to trickle down her throat. When she had had enough he drank himself, taking deep gulps of the water. Slowly the rhythm of his heartbeat began to steady. As he stood watching her she pulled the Roman cloak up higher, covering her face.

With one last, anxious look around he gathered the reigns of the donkey. They travelled at a slow pace, the donkey with head hanging low, refusing to be hurried, and the dog trailing behind. All the while his mind seethed with thoughts about the foolishness of what he was doing. He decided to skirt the village and take the longer route back to his house in the hope of avoiding any possible meetings.

Chapter Eight

The afternoon was well advanced when Tobiah arrived home with dried mud caking on his sandals and around the hem of his tunic. He drove the donkey into the field to graze and then lifted Leah from the cart to carry her into the house. On the threshold he hesitated for a moment, before crossing the floor to the bedroom and shouldering aside the curtain covering the doorway. With a deep sigh he laid her on the mattress and took a step back, his body becoming hunched and tense as he scrubbed the back of his hand across his parched lips. Her right hand was still tightly closed across her breast, concealing whatever it was she was holding, and his mind reeled at the enormity of what he had done.

From the courtyard he heard the dog bark a warning that a visitor had arrived and he was propelled into action. Quickly he tugged the cloak from around her and bundled it beneath the mattress. Ignoring her weak protests he covered her with a blanket and pulled it up over her head as he heard Malachi calling out his name.

Moments later he was standing framed in the doorway, a short, stocky man approaching sixty-five, with a mane of thick white hair.
The dog was pushing at the back of his legs, nudging him forward into the room, and he laughed, good-naturedly, as he bent and scratched behind its ears.

'Welcome home, Tobiah,' he said, with a broad smile. 'I expected you long before now. Miriam has been to the well and filled your water jar and left you bread that she baked herself this morning.' His eyes shone with his obvious pride and affection for his daughter. 'I have just been to visit your grandmother. She is waiting for you to join her for supper. Did you manage to sell...?'

His question remained unasked as a low moan came from beneath the blanket on the bed. As it was pushed aside the arm of a woman, mottled with fresh bruising appeared. Slowly her clenched fist opened and a large emerald ring dropped out and rolled across the floor. With another soft moan she pushed the blanket down further revealing her face. The gold bangles on her wrist gleamed, as they caught a shaft of sunlight filtering through a crack in the wooden blind covering the window.

Immobilized with shock Malachi stared down at her, all the warmth and friendliness disappearing from his face. He took a step back and the dog, sensing the crackling tension that had sprung up between the two men, moved to Tobiah's side.

'Malachi, it's not what you think.'

'It's not my place to think Tobiah. I'll go now. When you are ready we need to discuss the arrangements for the barley harvest.'

His expression hardened and there was a coldness about him that Tobiah had not seen before. He turned to leave and then stopped to look back over his shoulder.

'Don't keep Ahava waiting,' he said, his voice betraying his distress. 'She is eager to see you and hear about Matthias and Martha's child.'

Tobiah's face was filled with desperation as he stretched out a hand towards him.

'Don't go. Please, Malachi.'

He reached beneath the mattress and tugged out the red cloak, holding it up. Malachi took a quick, hissing intake of breath, and swung round to face him, running his fingers through his hair until it stood on end.

'What have you got yourself involved in, Tobiah? Is that what I think it is, a Roman cloak?'

Exhausted with fear and unable to answer, Tobiah swayed on his feet. Malachi moved swiftly to his side and thrust him forward.

'Go into the other room and sit down before you fall down,' he ordered, his tone gruff but not without affection.

With dreamlike slowness Tobiah made his way towards the table and lowered himself carefully onto a stool. Malachi padded after him and with trembling hands poured out two cups of wine, slopping it over the sides. Stern faced he took a long drink from one of the cups before sitting down and pushing the other towards Tobiah. Never in his life had he seen Malachi look so grim or so afraid. He lifted the wine cup and drained it, drips falling onto his tunic in spreading crimson stains.

'All right, start at the beginning,' Malachi said, firmly. 'Tell me how you come to have a half-dead woman in your bed, wearing gold bangles and clutching an emerald ring in her hand.' He banged his fist hard on the table. 'And what appears to be a centurion's cloak hidden beneath the mattress.'

Tobiah flinched and in a breaking voice he began to speak. When there was nothing else left to say he folded his arms across his chest and lowered his head. The silence that followed rested heavily between them until Malachi rose from his seat and began to pace the floor, stopping abruptly as he came to a decision.

'You need to wash and change your tunic. It's covered in mud and wine stains. Then you must to go and visit you grandmother. She will be getting anxious.'

'I can't leave the woman here alone.'

Malachi poured them each another cup of wine and sat down again, hitching his stool closer.

'I'll stay and talk to her. We need to hear her story. When you return we will decide together what to do.'

'Thank you! I don't know how I can ever repay you,' Tobiah said. He sagged with relief and Malachi gripped his arm hard.

'Listen to me carefully. In befriending this woman you may have put yourself in grave danger from the authorities. The ring she dropped and those bangles on her arm look to be worth a fortune. As for the cloak and whoever it is lying buried beneath that tree…' He paused and raked his beard. 'Just make sure Ahava doesn't become suspicious. The worry will be too much for her. You are not the best at hiding your feelings when you're anxious about something.' He tried to laugh but failed.

After Tobiah had left he sat drumming his fingers on the table, brooding. With a heavy sigh he pushed back his stool, straightening his shoulders as he stood. For a moment he hesitated, his lips pursed, then he walked briskly towards the room where Leah lay. He smiled grimly as he noticed that the ring was no longer lying on the floor and the bangles had disappeared from her wrist.

As he stood over her a look of puzzled concentration appeared on his face. There was something familiar about her and yet that was impossible. The only women he had ever known were those who lived in the village. Slowly a memory began to stir uneasily in his mind.

'Open your eyes and sit up,' he commanded. 'I know that you're awake.'

She struggled to raise herself, and as she looked at him he drew a sharp breath, because there was no mistaking those beautiful, mesmerizing eyes.

'Leah!'

'Yes, Malachi,' she whispered, through parched, cracked lips.

Her voice was lower and deeper than he remembered but then she had been just a girl, the same age as Miriam, when he had last seen her. His eyes widened in shock.

'Leah,' he said again, more softly.

'Yes, Malachi.'

Quickly he left the room, returning moments later with a cup of water and a stool, which he placed by the side of the bed. He sat down and offered her the water, holding the cup to her lips. When she had drunk her fill he put the cup on the floor and pushed a cushion behind her back. Gently he placed his large calloused hands over hers.

Despite her crushing grief for Daniel and the throbbing in her head from the wound, she felt warmed by the touch of this man who had so often befriended her as a child and whom she had loved like a father.

'What happened to you Leah? How did you come to end up in a field, next to a makeshift grave, and wrapped in a Roman cloak? And who is it lying in that grave?'

'My son Daniel.'

He gasped with shock and despite the threat her presence posed, a deep feeling of protectiveness towards her overwhelmed him. She pulled her hands free and bent forward, hiding her face behind her blood-matted curtain of hair. A tic began to beat in the corner of his left eye as he watched her.

'How did he die, Leah?'

She raised her head and pushed back her hair.

'He was murdered.'

His face darkened with anger as she told him what had happened to her, from the day that Marcellus bought her and her son, until the centurion left her by the side of Daniel's grave. When she finished she gave a deep sigh and lay back. Impulsively he stroked her face where the scar was and her eyes flickered open to meet his.

'Don't worry Malachi. I promise you, no trouble will follow me to Sychar. I am of no interest to the centurion.'

Although her voice held a note of conviction it did nothing to ease his worry.

'I hope you are right, Leah, because if you are not the consequences don't bear thinking about.'

An uneasy silence settled between them until he gently touched her hand.

'Who was Daniel's father Leah, and how did you both end up in slavery?'

'It doesn't matter who his father was, because he's dead. But I will tell you this, it was his fault we were sold into slavery.'

He watched her with helpless pity as she sat up and wrapped her arms around her body.

'Malachi, are my mother and father still alive?'

'No Leah, Joseph is dead and so is your sister Judith and her husband.'

She had thought nothing could ever cause her to feel pain again She had been wrong. The news of her sister's death tore through her.

'But my mother, Ahava, she is still alive?'

'Yes, she is.'

She gave a strained, hollow laugh that unnerved him.

'I would never have tried to return to Sychar had I thought for one moment that either she or my father might still be living,' she said bitterly.

Malachi shook his head in angry bewilderment.

'Your mother and father were not to blame for what happened to you all those years ago. How could they have known when they arranged your marriage that things would turn out so badly? They thought they had made a good match for you.'

She turned her head away but not before he had seen the bleak despair etched on her face.

'Look at me, Leah.'

Reluctantly she met his eyes.

'It broke Ahava's heart when she found out you had run away from your husband and that you were staying with Judith and

Thomas and refusing to see her or your father. It was cruel, especially as they were still mourning the death of your brother Reuben. Now that you have come back again, will you make your peace with her? She is old and nearing the end of her life.'

'No, I will not.'

Shocked and confused by her uncompromising bluntness Malachi struggled to control his anger.

'I don't understand you. Isn't it enough that your mother has lost two of her children to plague and is now widowed? How can you go on bearing this grudge towards her, after all these years? '

She didn't answer and he stared down at his tightly clasped hands as he recalled the silent, withdrawn and strangely watchful child she had once been. He realised then that there was nothing to be gained by pressing her further.

'I need to tell you, Leah.' he paused as he struggled to control the tremor in his voice. 'The man who found you is Tobiah, your sister's son. And this is his home.'

Her eyes widened with a look of stunned surprise. Stern faced and unblinking Malachi held her gaze.

'But he is not Judith's son, is he? He's mine,' she whispered.

'No, Leah! He is the son of Judith and Thomas. He was their child from the moment that you left him with them.'

'You know it wasn't because I didn't love him or want him,' she said, her voice breaking. 'I gave him to them because they were childless and I had no means of caring for him after I had run away from my husband. I was just sixteen Malachi and Tobiah needed a mother and a father,' she said pitifully, twisting the blanket in her hands. 'The day I left him with them I thought I would never recover from the pain. And I never did. But I took comfort from knowing he would always be safe with my sister and her husband because they would love him as though he were their own.'

'And they did, Leah. But it is not true you had no means of caring for him. You could have returned to the home of your mother and father or stayed with Judith and Thomas. They would have helped you raise Tobiah and you would have had the protection of us all, if your husband had come in search of you. Your sister was frantic with worry because you were so obstinately determined not to remain in Sychar. I didn't understand you then and I don't now.'

He saw her wince at the anger in his voice and he softened his tone.

'I only made arrangements for you to travel to Caesarea, with my brother Samuel, and his wife, to give Judith and your parents some peace of mind. Your mother and father never really recovered after you left Sychar without speaking to them. Their one consolation was that they were able to see their grandson and...'

He stopped, shocked by the expression of naked fury on her face and clenched his hands tightly in his lap, his knuckles showing white.

'And when a year later I got news that Samuel and Mary had died in a blaze that had burned down their home I believed you too had died with them.'

She stared at him, the anger leaving her, and a dry sob caught in her throat.

'I didn't know they were dead. I was only with them for four months. I grew to love them both dearly during that time.'

'If you loved them so much why did you leave their protection and the home and work they provided for you?' he asked sharply. 'Although it was as well you did or you wouldn't be alive now. Where did you go?'

'I don't want to talk about where I went,' she said wearily. 'But I will tell you this, it would have been better if I had died in that fire.'

He drew back as though he had been struck.

'I am deeply sorry, Leah, for all that has befallen you and for the murder of your son,' he said softly.

His anger she had understood but this gentle kindness was more than she could bear. She screwed her eyes tight in an attempt to stem the rising tide of pain and despair that was threatening to overwhelm her.

'Not one son, Malachi, I have lost two sons, haven't I? 'Did no one ever tell Tobiah that my sister and her husband were not his real parents?'

'No, Leah, they did not. Many children in the countryside are orphaned and taken in by their relatives and become the child of that family. From the moment you left Tobiah with Judith he became her and Thomas's son. When they both died of plague, eight years later, he went to live with his grandparents and became Tobiah, grandson of Joseph and Ahava.'

Her eyes darkened and once more the look on her face chilled him. For a while neither of them spoke, then with a deep, sigh he took her hands in his.

'If you are truly determined not to be reconciled with your mother, then it is kinder she doesn't discover you are here. Tobiah has gone to visit her. When he returns I'll tell him I think it for the best we find you some other village to settle in.

He paused, watching her in silence.

'What is it Malachi?'

'Are you going to tell him that you are his mother?'

'No, you have no need to worry. I wasn't coming to Sychar to claim him. I gave away that right all those years ago.' Despite her resolve to remain strong her voice broke. 'But I did long to see the man he had become. Does my mother believe I died in that fire?' she asked abruptly.

'Yes, she does. Reconsider Leah. Let me prepare her and then go and see her and make your peace.'

Silently she shook her head.

'Then we must let the past remain where it is. I have one more question and then you can rest. To whom do the ring and bangles belong?'

'They belong to me. They were presents from Marcellus.' She began to cry.

'I had to ask, Leah,' he said, when she had quietened. 'You didn't need to hide them. No one here will steal them from you.'

'I know that. And I'm sorry. Esther is a very lucky woman, Malachi. You have always provided for her and protected her. I wish…'

'What do you wish, Leah?'

She shook her head. 'It doesn't matter. Nothing can be altered by wishing.'

He stood and pulled the blanket up, tucking it around her shoulders, and then went to sit once more at the table, resting his head on his folded arms.

Chapter Nine

In Ahava's house there was a palpable tension. Ever alert to the moods of her grandson, it wasn't long after his arrival before she began to suspect something was wrong. The more she tried to draw him out the more evasive and withdrawn he became and the more her feeling of impending disaster increased.

As he began to sense her mounting anxiety he made an effort to lighten the atmosphere by telling her about Matthias's happiness with Martha and their baby, and the city gossip. None of it eased her mind. He was relieved when he could finally leave and walk out into the cool evening air.

As made his way home he wrestled with his thoughts. How long ago it seemed since he had stood on Matthias's roof in the moonlight, and how distant now his newfound feeling of peace felt. He was aware that his grandmother had not been deceived by his claims that everything was well and he was angry with himself for his weakness, and for not being more reassuring.

When he entered the house Malachi looked up, his eyes puffy with sleep. Without speaking he sat down beside him and the silence lengthened uncomfortably between them, until he could bear it no longer. He nodded his head in the direction of the room where Leah lay.

'Have you managed to speak with her?'

'Yes, I have.'

'And.'

Malachi rubbed his eyes until they became red and watery and gave a soft sigh.

'She's a runaway slave.'

Tension gripped the muscles in Tobiah's shoulders and his neck, and his head began to ache. He lent across the table for the jug of wine and re-filled their empty cups, pushing one towards Malachi and quickly draining his own.

'How did she come to be wrapped in a Roman Cloak and lying across a dead body?' His hand shook as he poured out another cup of wine.

After a moments hesitation Malachi told him what had happened to Leah and her son at the hands of the Roman and Tobiah's expression grew grim as he listened.

'I can vouch for the fact that he's dead. There was talk about it in the city yesterday.' A puzzled frown creased his forehead. 'Did she say why she and her son were making their way towards Sychar?'

Malachi avoided meeting his eyes, and Tobiah had a sudden inexplicable surge of apprehension about what he might tell him. When he finally spoke his voice was pitched so low that he had to lean forward to hear him.

'I know why, and I know who she is.'

Tobiah fought down a hysterical desire to laugh. 'You do! Who is she? How do you know her?'

'Her name is Leah and she's your mother's sister. She and her son were hoping to seek refuge with her.'

Tobiah stared at him in bewilderment.

'My mother didn't have a sister.'

'Yes, she did.'

'Grandmother has never spoken of her. Nor did my mother.' He scraped back his stool and stood up, his frustration spilling over. 'You had better explain. And I want the truth.'

'I am not in the habit of lying,' Malachi said harshly. 'Calm yourself, and sit down.'

He lifted his wine cup and drank deeply, then wiped his mouth with the back of his hand, his expression guarded.

'Leah was just thirteen when your grandparents arranged for her to marry a man who lived in a village in northern Samaria. Almost three years later she came back to the home of your mother and father, beaten and starved. Your mother and Esther looked after her. When she recovered we were all shocked by her determination not to stay in Sychar. Short of locking her up there was no way we could stop her leaving. For her safety I arranged for her to go to Caesarea with my brother and his wife who were going to live there. She refused to see your grandparents before she left and she is refusing to see Ahava now.'

'I don't understand.'

Malachi gnawed on the skin at the side of his thumbnail until it bled.

'Neither do I. I think she blames your grandmother for what happened to her at the hands of her husband. So, for Ahava's sake, it is best she doesn't find out that she is here.'

For a long while Tobiah remained silent, his mind feverishly going over what Malachi had told him. With a growing certainty he felt that something was being hidden from him. There was a strange nervousness in Malachi's manner that he had never seen before.

'How did she and her son come to be sold into slavery?'

'I don't know. The house my brother and his wife were living in burned down. When we got the news we thought Leah had died with them in the fire. She refuses to say what happened to her, or who the father of her son is.'

'I think I must tell my grandmother that her daughter is here in the village,' Tobiah said, with a look of defiance that was unusual in him.

Malachi banged his fist down hard on the table in exasperation.

'No, you will not. Nor will you tell anyone else. Although Leah says the centurion will not come looking for her we cannot be sure of it. The fewer people who know about her, the safer it will be for all of us. There are serious legal penalties for harbouring a runaway slave.'

Tobiah stared at him in amazement, a rising tide of hot anger sweeping over him.

'I think you forget yourself. I will make the decisions not you.'

Malachi shook his head and rose to his feet, his face set in lines of determination. 'Not this time! We need to get Leah settled in some other village as soon as possible. Your grandmother believes she is dead. To tell her the daughter she loved is alive and has come home again, but is still refusing to see her, would surely be too much for her to bear.'

Ashamed of his outburst Tobiah grasped his arm. 'I'm sorry. Forgive me.'

Malachi's voice softened. 'There is nothing to forgive. We are both tired. Tomorrow things will look better. You were careful to make sure Ahava didn't suspect anything was wrong?'

The answer was clear on Tobiah's face even before he spoke.

'You know how she is. I was hardly across the threshold before she sensed something and began questioning me. I told her that I was just weary from the journey. But I don't think I convinced her.'

'Well it can't be helped now. You will have to try to dispel any fears she may have when next you see her. When I get home I will speak with Esther and ask if she will allow Miriam to come tomorrow to look after Leah.'

Tobiah gasped. 'You can't involve Esther and Miriam!'

'There is no other way. Leah needs a woman to look after her until she is recovered enough to leave Sychar. Neither you nor I can do that. The village has grown used to my wife and daughter bringing food and doing household tasks for you since Rebekah died. No one will suspect anything by the comings and goings of either of them.'

Reluctantly Tobiah nodded and lent back watching him through half closed eyes.

'And there is nothing more you should tell me?'

'No!'

'Then tomorrow I shall return to the field where her son lies and take him to our family tomb. He's my cousin. I won't leave his body to be eaten by wild animals.'

Malachi grasped his arm and the tic at the corner of his left eye began beating rapidly again.

'Is it not enough that you have brought Leah to your home, at great danger to yourself and the village, without taking any more risks?'

'No! My son lived for only a few hours but the pain of his death is made more bearable because he lies with his mother and his ancestors.' His voice began to tremble. 'This woman, my aunt, appears to have suffered greatly. It may give her comfort to know that her son is buried with his family.'

'Then you are not going alone. If you are determined to do this I shall go with you.'

The two men clasped hands, and Malachi flexed his shoulders that had become stiff with tension.

'I must go home now. Esther will be getting anxious and I need to tell her about Leah and where we will be going tomorrow.'

'What will you tell Miriam?'

For a long moment Malachi remained silent. 'I can't tell her the truth,' he said finally. 'She will have to be told you found an injured woman on the road, lying beside her dead son, and that they had been attacked by robbers. I will also warn her that she is not to say anything about her to Ahava or anyone else in the village.'

'She will be curious as to why we are keeping her a secret and going to bury the body of her son.'

Malachi gave a soft laugh. 'Miriam knows you have a kind heart Tobiah. She will not be surprised, as I am not, by the things you do.' His expression sobered. 'She is a good, obedient daughter. She knows better than to ask questions. She will do, as she always does, exactly as she is told.'

Their eyes met and held, then Malachi smiled and took Tobiah by his shoulders.

'I'll be here tomorrow at daybreak. Try and get some sleep.'

Chapter Ten

Tobiah was hitching the donkey to the cart as the sun rose, gilding the tops of the mountains and lighting up the valley through the milky haze of the early dawn. Within minutes Malachi was walking towards him, his footsteps making deep impressions in the dew drenched grass. He raised a hand in acknowledgement and smiled. The strain of the previous day had disappeared from his face and Tobiah felt his spirits begin to rise as he returned his greeting.

'Did you manage to sleep, Tobiah?'

'Yes. Well, fitfully. He gave a harsh laugh. 'For a short while yesterday I had begun to feel that my life might have regained some purpose and meaning, but now everything is in turmoil.' He paused. 'There is something I want to ask you.'

'What?'

'No, not now, we will talk later, when we get home.'

Malachi shrugged and tossed the two white sheets he was carrying into the cart then, for a while, he stood wrapped in thought, looking out across the fields towards Mount Gerizim. As he turned back towards Tobiah he placed a hand on his shoulder.

'Take heart, Tobiah. It is a good thing that we do now. Have you spoken with Leah this morning?'

'No,' Tobiah snapped, unreasonably irritated by the probing anxiety in Malachi's voice. 'When I looked in on her she was sleeping. I left fruit and water for her.'

'Good, she will need that when she wakes. Esther has agreed Miriam can come later to look after her and prepare a meal for our return. She said we deserve a special treat for when we get back. A stew of chicken and vegetables, I think.' He laughed and rubbed his hands together ignoring the dark look on Tobiah's face.

'Was Esther shocked when you told her about Leah?'

Malachi face sobered. 'Yes, she was. But she agrees we must do all we can to help her. Although she too thinks we should find her somewhere else to settle. As quickly as possible,' he added carefully.

Without replying Tobiah began leading the donkey forward with the dog at his heels.

They followed the path through the olive grove and left the village behind, walking in silence, neither having much appetite for conversation. As the morning wore on and the sun became hotter they shed their cloaks. An hour later Tobiah called a halt and Malachi passed him one of the water skins he had filled. Whilst they drank he stared into the distance, a deep frown furrowing his forehead. Tobiah leant on the side of the cart watching him through half closed eyes, wondering what he was thinking.

'If we set off now and can get this animal to move a little faster we should be there within the hour,' he said.

With an absent-minded nod, Malachi picked up the reigns of the reluctant donkey, coaxing him forward. It was unusual for him to remain so silent and brooding and it added to Tobiah's sense of unease. He chewed on his lip as he mulled over their conversation of the previous evening, unable to rid himself of the feeling that there had been something evasive in Malachi's manner.

'I don't know why, but I feel there is more to Leah than you have been willing to tell me,' he said, unable to contain himself any longer.

With an expression of pained exasperation Malachi brought the donkey to a halt. He was facing the sun and he squinted across at Tobiah, shading his eyes with his hand.

'I told you last night and I will tell you again, for the last time. You have her story exactly as she told it to me.'

'And there is nothing else?'

'No,' Malachi said without meeting his eyes.

Tobiah knew that to question him further would yield nothing more and yet still the feeling persisted.

'Tell me about my aunt,' he said softly. 'What was she like as a child?'

There was a long silence and he could see from the smile playing at the corners of Malachi's mouth, and the far-away look on his face, that he was somewhere back in the past.

'She was a lovely child, taller than most of her age, but delicate and graceful,' he said slowly. 'She didn't speak much but she watched everyone with those beautiful eyes that somehow always seemed filled with such sadness. When she wasn't following me around the farm she was trailing after your mother and Esther. Rarely did she play with the other children in the village.'

'I don't understand why my grandfather didn't insist she return to live under his roof after she ran away from her husband, instead of allowing her to leave Sychar with your brother and his wife.'

'Joseph hadn't been the same since your uncle Reuben died and Ahava too had not been well. Perhaps he thought it for the best,' Malachi said sharply, determined he would not to be drawn into any further discussion about Leah.

They were both startled when the dog barked. With its stump of a tail wagging furiously it bounded towards a rocky outcrop in pursuit of a rabbit that quickly disappeared into a burrow. Both men looked at each other in surprised amusement. Malachi threw back his head and laughed and Tobiah joined in, the tension between them easing as they watched the animal lope sheepishly back towards them.

For the next mile the track narrowed and the terrain became hillier. Tobiah fell behind, leaving Malachi leading the donkey until they reached the open plain When they came within sight of the tree, beneath which Daniel's body lay, two birds of prey were circling high above. Tobiah felt an ache begin deep in his chest as Malachi took the linen cloths from the cart.

With slow deliberation they walked towards the makeshift grave. Some of the smaller stones had been scattered and the foot that he had seen protruding was gone; all that remained were stains of dried blood and a few splintered bones and animal droppings.

Malachi spread one of the sheets on the ground close to the grave. Dropping down they knelt on it and leaned back on their haunches, the silence broken only by the ominous call of the birds still circling above. Almost in unison they began removing the debris left by the storm and then the soil and stones, to reveal the rotting corpse beneath. The body had been lying in the heat for almost three days and the odour was overpowering. Tobiah stood and turned away to vomit. Malachi quickly rolled Daniel onto the sheet, wrapping it tightly around him and winding the other from his feet to his head. Reverently they lifted him and carried him to the waiting cart, grateful that the surrounding countryside was empty of travellers. In silence they reached for their water skins and washed their hands.

The burial ground lay towards Mount Ebal and they were making good progress when Malachi drew the donkey to a halt. They watched, in silence, as a small caravan, heralded by a tinkling bell, wound its way in their direction, Quickly Malachi threw his cloak over the body in the cart and cast a warning glance at Tobiah, who followed with his cloak. It took a moment before they recognised the two men walking alongside the camels as travelling merchants from Gerasa in the Decapolis. They had many times taken lodgings at the farm on their way home from selling their goods in the markets and fairs throughout the province.

With his face creasing into a smile of recognition, the man holding the leading rein brought the heavily laden camels to a halt. As he walked towards them Tobiah lifted his hand in salute.

'Greetings Simeon.'

'Greetings Tobiah, this is an unusual place to find you at harvest time. I thought you would be in the fields.' He raised an eyebrow, and there was more than a hint of curiosity in his voice.

The dog growled softly and Tobiah gave a forced laugh as Malachi moved to his side.

'We finished the barley harvest three days ago and we're on our way home after selling the surplus grain in the city.'

He was shocked with the ease at which the lie had come to his lips, and he caught Malachi looking sideways at him with a flash of amused admiration in his eyes.

Simeon's expression was one of open disbelief as he gazed down at what lay in the cart, covered by their cloaks.

'I'll let you continue on your journey then,' he said, looking up and signalling to his companion to move on. 'We are going first to the market in Sebaste and then on to Galilee. On our way home we'll take lodgings in your barn for a night, if we may? Any goods we have left over we may be able to sell in the village before we leave.'

Tobiah bowed low in mock solemnity. 'It will be my pleasure to accommodate you.'

'Kill and roast a lamb, Tobiah, and let us hope it smells better than whatever it is you're hiding in that cart,' Simeon said, pressing his hand over his nose and mouth in an exaggerated gesture of disgust.

Greatly relieved that they were leaving without further questions, Tobiah smiled and nodded.

'It will be the fattest in the flock and I will uncork my finest wines.'

As the camels moved off the laughter of the men rang out and Malachi slapped Tobiah on the back.

'That was quick thinking Tobiah.' He paused and a cautious note entered his voice. 'Although I'm sure neither of them believed you. They will have passed your grain fields an hour ago and seen they have yet to be harvested.'

Tobiah surprised himself by laughing. 'No, they knew I was lying. But fortunately they were more concerned with continuing on their journey than finding out the truth. I've no doubt when they return from trading their goods Simeon will question me further,' he said ruefully.

'Just stick to the same story. It will be too late for him to unravel it by then. I really didn't know you had it in you to think so quickly, and to lie so well.'

Tobiah looked at him in silence for a moment.

'Nor did I Malachi, nor did I. I seem to be discovering new things about myself all the time. Some of them I don't like.'

With his own face now mirroring the seriousness of Tobiah's, Malachi placed a hand on his shoulder.

'You are a good man, Tobiah. Don't judge yourself so harshly. Come, our journey's almost over.'

When they reached the burial ground, and the tomb of Tobiah's family, that had been hewn out of the side of a rock, they began to roll away the large boulder covering the entrance. After it was done they walked in silence to the cart. Between them they reverently lifted the body of Daniel and slowly made their way back to the tomb, where they laid him down on a stone slab. As they stood motionless at the entrance, with their heads bowed, Malachi recited a verse from scripture. They rolled back the boulder and leaned against it. Malachi was the first to recover and he took Tobiah's arm.

'We have done all we can for now. We can come back when the flesh has rotted from Daniel's body to put his bones in a casket and lay them beside his ancestors. We need to find some shade now and rest for a while before we go home.'

Chapter Eleven

The remainder of their journey back to Tobiah's house was uneventful. It was with a sigh of relief that he unhitched the donkey and drove it into the field. As he and Malachi made their way towards the front of the house, the smell of stewing meat and baking bread drifted towards them. Tobiah rubbed his hands together.

'I can't remember when I last felt so hungry or when food smelled so good. I am glad that you are staying to eat with me, Malachi, I need your company for a while. There is something I want to ask you.'

Before an intrigued Malachi could respond Miriam appeared framed in the doorway. Flushed from preparing the meal, and with a shy smile touching the corners of her lips, she took her father's hand and kissed his cheek. Glancing sideways at Tobiah she allowed her smile to widen, and then she laughed.

'I am glad to see you both,' she said softly. 'I have your meal ready.'

She removed her hand from Malachi's and looked down at the dog.

'I'll get a bowl of water for this creature too,' she said. 'It looks as though it needs some.'

Tobiah felt his heartbeat quicken, and a lifting of his spirits that almost made him dizzy. Swiftly, and impulsively, he crossed the courtyard with long strides to pick a flower from a heavily laden Myrtle bush. The flush on his face almost matched hers as he pressed it into her hand. She looked directly up at him, her eyes dancing with delight at the unexpectedness of the gift. The moment was broken as Malachi coughed.

'Let us go inside, Miriam,' he said ushering her forward. 'Tobiah and I need to talk with you about the woman you have been caring for today.'

Resentful of the change in atmosphere, brought about by her father's words, Miriam wore a sulky frown as she walked into the house, followed closely by the two men. Unaware of his daughter's displeasure, Malachi sat down at the table and patted the stool at his side.

'Come and sit by me, Miriam' he said, smiling. 'You have been working hard and you must be tired.'

'One moment, father.'

Her frown had quickly disappeared, to be replaced with a smile. She put the flower down and lifted a jug from the shelf to fill a bowl with water. Bending gracefully she placed it on the floor for the dog and tilted her head to one side. With a hand resting on her hip she watched as it lapped noisily. Tobiah thought he had never seen her look more beautiful. Still smiling she turned towards her father.

'Before I answer your questions let me pour some wine to refresh you both.' She raised her eyebrows and wagged her finger at them. 'Although you should both have washed the dust from you first,' she said, imitating her mother's voice and manner.

Tobiah laughed and his eyes followed her as she brought two cups to the table and filled them to the brim with wine. With mock solemnity Malachi turned towards him as he sat down.

'This is the thanks a father gets for being too lenient, a wilful daughter who orders him about and does as she pleases and not as she is told. She will be the bane of my old age. Now Miriam, tell us how the woman you have been caring for has been.'

Deliberately choosing not to sit on the stool by her father, Miriam remained standing with her hands clasped demurely.

'When I arrived this morning Leah was sleeping,' she said.

'She told you her name?' he interrupted, his tone harsher than he intended, and Tobiah gave him a warning look.

'I asked her what it was. I had to call her something,' she said nervously.

Malachi lent forward, returning Tobiah's look. Then he sank back, pursing his lips. Noticing the unspoken exchange between the two men Miriam's eyes gleamed with interest.

'As I was saying, she was still sleeping. I feared she might be dead because she was so still and quiet. But then she stirred and moaned a little. After a moment she opened her eyes and looked at me. Such beautiful, unusual eyes.' She put a hand to her cheek. 'But that awful scar,' she said softly.

Tobiah shifted uneasily and exchanged glances again with Malachi wishing that he could read what was going on in his mind.

'Go on, daughter,' Malachi urged.

'I told her that I had come to help her and she tried to smile at me. Although I am sure her poor head must have been hurting very much from the wound at the back. I gave her some of mother's medicine and she lay down to rest again. It was a while before I heard her stir. I took in a bowl of water and towels and helped her remove her clothes.'

She glanced at Tobiah and then lowered her eyes. 'I'd brought a clean tunic for her and a sash and a veil. Everything she was wearing was dirty and stained with blood. She allowed me to bathe her and clean the wound on her head and I combed her hair a little. Afterwards she drank some of the goats milk that Caleb had brought earlier.'

She swayed gently on her feet and there was a dreamy, sensual look about her that caused Tobiah to feel suddenly discomfited.

'I invited him into the house and gave him a cup of water before he went back to the herd,' she said, her voice almost too low to be heard.

As she caught the look of shock that passed between her father and Tobiah she realised what she had let slip and she bit down on her bottom lip. Her voice shook as she struggled to regain her composure and her words tumbled out in a rush.

'An hour before you arrived home I managed to persuade her to drink a little wine mixed with water and eat a small piece of cheese and bread. Afterwards she had some fruit and honey.'

She looked down and when she lifted her head Tobiah caught his breath at the sweet earnestness in her face.

'Mother had given me a sleeping potion for her and I mixed it with her drink. She is resting comfortably now.'

Malachi again exchanged looks with Tobiah and she held her breath.

'You have done well Miriam.' Despite his praise she trembled at his stern expression.

'Now, tell me, how many times have you invited the goat herder into the house when you have been here alone?'

She opened her eyes wide, forcing them to fill with tears as her mind raced.

'Only this once. He said he felt unwell and it seemed a kindness to invite him in out of the heat and give him a drink. His water skin was empty and I filled it for him. I am sorry father.'

Lowering her head submissively she clasped her hands in front of her again. Malachi slammed his fist down on the table.

'I want the truth, Miriam. Did you mention the woman to Caleb? And what if she had got up, eh, and he had seen her?'

Nervously she looked from her father to Tobiah.

'She was asleep and I didn't say a word about her to him.' Her face flushed and the tears spilled onto her cheeks. 'You and mother told me that I wasn't to speak to anyone about her, and I haven't. Caleb was only in the house for a short while.'

Malachi raked at his beard as he stared at her.

'He shouldn't have been in the house alone with you for any length of time,' he said angrily.

Tobiah laid a restraining hand on his arm. 'No harm has been done, Malachi. Miriam was acting out of kindness and they weren't really alone.' He gestured towards the room where Leah lay. 'But I will have a word with Caleb tomorrow and warn him it mustn't happen again.'

He smiled at them both and as Miriam gave him a look of gratitude he fought the urge to take her in his arms and kiss her.

For a few moments longer Malachi remained ill humoured, his face masked by a deep frown. Then he stood and put an arm around his daughter's shoulders. He had never been able to remain angry with her for long and his expression softened as she looked up at him with wide-eyed innocence.

'You are just like your mother,' he said quietly. 'Always trying to befriend someone.'

Much relieved, she recovered quickly and exchanged another smile with Tobiah from the shelter of her father's arm. She allowed her eyes to linger briefly on his before lowering her head and glancing up again, with a quick sideways look, from beneath her fringe of lashes. Her lips had parted slightly and Tobiah sat mesmerised by the small, pink tip of her tongue, just visible, and he felt his body stir. He picked up his wine cup and drank deeply, holding her in a steady gaze.

Oblivious to the scene being played out between Tobiah and his daughter, Malachi sat down again.

'Did Leah tell you anything about herself, Miriam?' he asked.

'No, only her name.'

Feeling surer of her ground now, she looked from her father to Tobiah. Her manner was so meek that any misgivings they may have had about her behaviour began to evaporate.

'Before I go home let me serve your meal,' she said lightly. 'Everything is ready. All I need do is ladle it out. But, first, both of you go and wash. Even your faces are streaked with dust.'

She laughed and Tobiah found himself laughing with her. Malachi took the towel she was holding out and they made their way to the rainwater cistern at the back of the house. She called after them to hurry and they smiled foolishly at each other, each happy for her to remain a little while longer.

By the time they returned, the oil lamps had been lit and the room had taken on a warm, comforting glow. After inviting them to sit down, she busied herself filling two bowls with a steaming stew and carried them to the table, followed by a plate of warm bread. Malachi got up and drew her to him and she laid her head on his breast.

'Go home now, Miriam, to your mother. Tell her I will be with her soon.'

For a moment longer she remained leaning against him and then she drew back. She looked at Tobiah and his breath caught in his throat. With a smile she inclined her head towards him and she was aware that his eyes were following her as she crossed the room.

As she disappeared through the doorway, it seemed to him that the light had dimmed a little. He topped up the wine cups and pushed one towards Malachi. Suddenly they both realised of how very hungry they were and they ate in silence until their bowls were empty. Leaning back in his chair, Malachi wiped his mouth and took a sip of his wine.

'You have said twice today that there was something you wanted to ask me. Is now the time?'

Tobiah rose from the table and scraped the leftovers from the cooking pot into a bowl for the dog.

'Yes, I think it is, and I think you may have guessed what I want to ask you.'

Malachi remained silent, his face impassive, and Tobiah was forced to continue.

'I would like your permission to take Miriam as my wife,' he said softly, as he sat down beside him again. 'And I promise you, Malachi, I will be a good husband to her.'

Malachi eyes were bright with unshed tears as he took Tobiah's hands in his.

'I have worked for your family ever since I was a boy, Tobiah. And over the years I have watched you grow into a fine man.'

He paused, his thoughts turning inwards and Tobiah waited patiently for him to continue.

'For many years, after our last son was born, Esther and I longed for another child. When all hope appeared gone we were blessed with the miracle of Miriam. There is nothing more we could want for her, than to have you as her husband.'

He drew himself up straight and clasped the younger man's hands in his, holding them firmly.

'I know that my daughter will consider it an honour to be your wife.'

He let go of Tobiah's hands and threw back his head, laughing loudly.

'I think from what I have seen my daughter is already more than a little in love with you.'

Tobiah smiled. 'I would not have asked for her if I had thought otherwise,' he said. As he spoke he felt a stirring of unease. He shrugged it aside and his face became earnest. 'I promise you, Malachi, I will take good care of her and if we are blessed with children, you and I will be joined by blood as well as well as friendship.'

Malachi nodded his head as he dashed the tears away that had spilled onto his cheeks.

'I will speak with Esther and then we must let your grandmother know. She will be delighted,' he said, breaking into a smile.

The two men rose from the table and Malachi placed his hands on Tobiah's shoulder.

'We both need some rest now. Tomorrow we begin the barley harvest. I have hired the labourers and they will be here early.' His face became sombre and Tobiah tensed.

'If Leah is up and about tell her to remain out of sight. We don't want word of her getting back to Ahava or any gossip spreading around the village. Esther will come and tend to her because Ahava will be expecting Miriam's help with the milling.'

Tobiah frowned. 'The work is getting too much for her and she doesn't need to do it.'

'She knows that Tobiah, but grinding the grain makes her feel useful and at her age that's important.' His eyes danced with amusement. 'When she hears the news about you and Miriam it will give her something else to think about. I have no doubt she will want to interfere in all the wedding arrangements.'

Both men laughed affectionately, knowing that Ahava would not be left out of the planning.

After Malachi had left Tobiah remained at the table, slowly sipping his wine, until he felt his eyes beginning to close. He stood and shook his head to clear it and looked towards the room where Leah lay, and a feeling of apprehension swept over him. Hastily he bundled up a sleeping mat and blanket and carried them to the roof, where he lay watching the stars until he fell asleep.

Chapter Twelve

After leaving Tobiah and her father enjoying their meal Miriam made her way through the olive grove towards the village. The late afternoon sun was filtering through the trees and dappling the path in front of her with shifting light, as the leaves stirred in the breeze. Smiling softly to herself she raised her arms and pulled her veil loose, shaking her head until her hair fell, thick and glossy, about her shoulders.

With a low, throaty laugh she started to run, her face suffused with excitement. She was certain now that her plan was succeeding and that Tobiah would soon be asking her father if they could become betrothed. At last, she thought, all these months of soft smiles and sideways looks, the carrying of water and the cooking of food and pretended concern for that miserable dog, were now going to be made worthwhile.

Half way down the track she paused, out of breath. A deepening flush was staining her cheeks and her eyes glittered. She pursed her lips and began imitating the soft, cooing sounds of a dove and then stood with her head tilted to one side, listening. When she heard the answering call a wide smile spread across her face. Almost instantly Caleb emerged from the trees. In long, bounding strides he quickly covered the space between them and stopped in front of her. Roughly he dragged her towards him, enveloping her in his arms and tumbling her to the ground. She bit his hand and kicked him, in an effort to break free, as he fought to pin her down and kiss her. Their noisy laughter sent a rush of birds fluttering from the trees.

He released her suddenly and jumped up to stand over her, sucking at the bite. With another loud laugh he lunged forward, grasping her arm and hauling her from the ground. He held her tight with one hand and tugged back her head with his other, until she was looking up at him, their faces inches apart.

'I brought the goats down from the hillside ages ago. I was almost asleep when I heard you call. Why have you been so long?'

'Because Tobiah and father were back later than expected, and then they wanted to talk to me about the woman I was looking after. Let me go.'

She kicked out at his ankles until he released her, only to press herself back into his arms, kissing him wildly. He pushed her away and held her from him by her shoulders. They stood gazing at each other, their eyes locked and their breath coming in quick, short gasps, until Miriam pulled free and wrinkled her nose.

'Ugh! You smell of goat,' she said, putting a hand across her face.

He grinned and nodded. 'Yes, I do. It's probably because I'm a goat herder.'

He tilted his head and narrowed his eyes, and his laugh was coarse as he took her back into his arms again.

'The smell has never bothered you before.'

She contorted her face into mock fierceness, raising a clench fist to hit him. He grabbed her wrist, holding it tight.

'Stop it now, Miriam, be calm. This is too dangerous. Your father may come along at any moment.'

'No, he won't.' Her voice rose with excitement. 'Sit down beside me Caleb. I have something important to tell you.'

She dragged him to the side of the path and dropped to the ground, resting her back against a tree. Caleb lay propped on one elbow at her feet, his eyes bright with curiosity.

'I think it is finally going to happen. Father and Tobiah are having a meal together and I'm certain Tobiah is going to ask him if we can become betrothed.' She twisted a lock of hair around her finger and her tone was mocking as she glanced sideways at him. 'I am sure my father will be only too delighted to say yes.'

'I'm sure he will too,' Caleb said bitterly, the light dying in his eyes. 'Tobiah's rich and he owns land. His family has lived here for generations. Not like me, a goat herder, who never knew his father and whose mother was a city prostitute.'

'You know it's you I want, not Tobiah,' she said, her tone wheedling. 'He's so pious and good and...' She wrinkled her nose and sat up straight. 'And so serious looking.'

Caleb felt a dull sinking in his chest. 'It doesn't matter what you want. Your father would never agree to you marrying me because I have nothing to offer you.'

He stared at her, fear etched on his face. 'Tobiah will know, Miriam. He will know on your wedding night that you are not a virgin.'

He looked so anxious that she took him in her arms, stroking his hair and soothing him as she would a child.

'Hush now! You know I have a plan. I shall make sure that he gets very drunk, and then I will slip one of mother's sleeping potions into his wine before we go to bed. When he's asleep and snoring I'll spread goats blood over the sheet as proof of my virginity. The next day he will be unable to remember anything that happened, because he will have such a headache,' she finished triumphantly.

He pulled free from her arms, conflicting emotions of fear and fascination crossing his face.

'I can't bear the thought of you marrying him Miriam. There will be other nights,' he said, his voice roughening with resentment.

Impatiently Miriam tossed her head and took his hands in hers, squeezing them hard.

'It will only be for a little while and it will mean nothing to me. We have discussed this over and over, Caleb. We need Tobiah's money if we are to escape from Sychar and build a new life together. I know he keeps a hoard somewhere around that house, although I have never been able to find it. Once he and I are married I will be able to persuade him to tell me where it's hidden.'

'I don't want to steal from him Miriam. Why can't we leave now and take our chances? I'll find work and protect you.' He gave her a sly, sideways look. 'Or you could search your father's house for any money he has hidden and take that. We would be able to leave then without you having to marry Tobiah.'

She stared at him for a moment, her eyes narrowing. 'I suppose there is the money that he's been saving over the years for my dowry. But I have no idea where he keeps it.' She shrugged her shoulders. 'And even if I manage to find it I know it won't be anywhere near enough for what we will need. My father isn't a wealthy man.'

She sucked on her thumb and Caleb knew from her expression that she was plotting something he wasn't going to like.

'I have an idea. We don't need to steal from anyone. When Tobiah and I are married I could poison his wine. Mother has taught me enough about plants for me to know which are safe to use for medicines and which are dangerous. When he dies I would be a rich widow and we could marry once the mourning period is over. The farm would be ours.'

Caleb leapt to his feet as though stung, screaming at her to stop. Miriam caught his had in a tight grip and pulled him back down, pinching him hard, fearful she had gone too far.

'Don't be stupid, Caleb. You know I wouldn't poison Tobiah. But we do need his money so that we can pay the boat price to Corinth and begin our new life there together.'

'Talking about it is one thing, doing it is something else,' he said sulkily. 'Corinth is in another country and so far away. I have never been on a boat before and I am frightened of the sea.'

Miriam scowled and pinched him again.

'Don't do that, Miriam,'

She laughed, cruelly. 'You are such a baby. There is nothing to be frightened of because I will be with you. And we will have a great deal of money in our purse.'

Caleb made a display of rubbing his arm.

'I told you I don't want to steal from Tobiah. I was hardly more than a child when he found me starving in the city after my mother had been murdered. I might have been taken as a slave, or worse, if he hadn't rescued me and persuaded his grandfather to give me work on the farm.'

'Oh do stop! Tobiah's a great collector of strays: wild dogs, orphaned boys, beaten women.' Her eyes bored into his. 'If stealing his money bothers you that much, I'll leave him some. Although I don't see why I should.' she said irritably.

'We shouldn't be taking any of it,' Caleb muttered. 'It's a sin to steal.'

'I know. But he will have taken me as his wife and I will deserve something for that. So it won't be a sin.' Her voice turned peevish. 'But what you and I have been doing together is a sin. And it will be a graver sin once Tobiah and I are betrothed. That doesn't seem to bother you though.'

Caleb's face turned ashen. 'It does bother me.'

Confused and frightened he stumbled over his words as he made a further attempt at deflecting her.

'If your plan doesn't work, and Tobiah discovers on your wedding night that you are not a virgin, your father will have you stoned to death for bringing disgrace on his family.' His voice trembled. 'I will be stoned too because you will be forced to say who the man was. We should go now, whilst we have the chance.'

'I've told you, he won't find out. And we are not going to run off without any money.' She appeared distracted and he watched her with apprehension, fearful of what might be coming next.

'Father and Tobiah know you came to the house today and stayed for a while, and they are angry about it.'

The sinking feeling in his chest returned. 'How do they know?'

'Because I let it slip. But don't worry. Tobiah came to the rescue persuading father it was because I have a kind heart that I invited you in to rest.' She laughed and nestled her head against his shoulder. 'If only they knew the truth!'

Caleb frowned.

'Listen to me,' she said, prodding his chest. 'Tobiah intends to speak with you tomorrow and warn you not to enter the house again when I am there alone. And he might try to find out if you know anything about the woman. So be on you guard.'

For a moment he looked anxious and then his lips twisted into a sneer.

'Ah yes! The mysterious woman who has appeared from nowhere, beaten and bruised and lying in Tobiah's bed, of all places. I would really like to know the truth about her.'

Miriam's face flushed with anger as she wrenched herself away from him. She caught his ear between her fingers and twisted hard, her voice rising to a shrill screech.

'You are not to tell anyone about her, do you hear me? I dread to think what father might do if he finds out I've told you about her.'

'Yes, I hear you. That hurt, Miriam.'

She cupped his face in her hands and kissed him and then she frowned. 'I am certain there's more to her than I've been told, because he and mother spent a long time whispering to each other after I had gone to bed. I tried hard to listen but their voices were too low. But I heard mother crying.'

'Why would she be crying, and why is your father so concerned about Tobiah? He's only a servant of his just like I am,' he said irritably.

'Don't talk such foolishness and don't sulk. It doesn't suit you.'

He glared at her.

'What if the woman was listening to us this morning when I took you on the floor? You always make such a noise Miriam. We shouldn't have discussed our plans either,' he said nervously.

'There's no need to worry. She couldn't have heard because mother made up a medicine for her, to help ease her pain and make her drowsy. When I looked in on her moments before you arrived she was sleeping soundly. And she was still sleeping after you left.'

She kissed him and burrowed into him, her body trembling as he felt for her under her tunic. Grabbing his wrist she pulled his hand away.

'No, not now, Caleb! I have to go. Mother will be wondering where I am. I will see you tomorrow.'

'It's getting too dangerous, Miriam. I think we should wait for a while.'

She held his gaze with a look that alarmed him.

'I don't want to wait. I shall be collecting herbs for mother's medicines tomorrow. So, meet me in the valley late in the afternoon, before you take the goats back to their pen for the night.'

With a shrug of resignation he rose from the ground. 'Have it your way, Miriam, you always do,' he said on a sigh.

He stepped back and stood looking down on her in a bewilderment of desire and fear. When he had disappeared into the olive grove she scrambled to her feet and fixed her veil over her head, brushing the dust and pieces of dried grass from her tunic as she began to run towards home.

As she neared the bottom of the track she saw her mother walking towards her, waving her hand. She felt a sharp stab of fear as she realised that the light was fading. Somehow she must think of a reason for arriving home so late because her mother was sure to tell her father she had been forced to come looking for her. She began to run, covering the distance between them quickly and throwing her arms around her.

'You had me worried Miriam, I expected you long before now,' Esther said sharply, breaking free of her daughter's arms. 'Surely Tobiah and your father haven't only just returned.'

'No, they have been back for quite a while. I am sorry to be so late.' With a shy smile at her mother she lowered her head and then looked quickly up at her again. 'Father wanted to talk to me about the woman I've been looking after and then I dawdled a bit on the way home. I know I shouldn't have but I sat down to think about something important and lost all sense of time.'

Esther laughed and lifted her daughter's chin; her anxiety disappearing as she looked into the sweet faced innocence of Miriam.

'What was so important, child?'

'I think Tobiah is about to ask father if we can become betrothed.'

Miriam's voice had risen excitedly. Holding her at arms length by her shoulders Esther shook her gently.

'What makes you think that, Miriam?'

'The way he has been looking at me recently and today he gave me a flower.'

Esther gave her a searching look. 'It's time Tobiah found another wife. And I know it would delight his grandmother and your father. But I am not sure giving you a flower means that he has chosen you. Is it what you want, Miriam?'

'Yes, it is. Especially when I think how much it would please everyone. I would be such a good wife to him,' she said, her eyes wide and shining.

Esther stroked her cheek and smiled. 'Well, we will just have to wait and see. Let us go home now, daughter.'

She slipped an arm around her waist and Miriam laid her head on her shoulder as they made their way towards the village.

Chapter Thirteen

On the following morning, an hour after sunrise, Malachi and Esther were on their way to Tobiah's house. They spoke in low whispers as they walked, despite the fact that there were only the birds and wild animals to hear them.

'I wasn't able to sleep last night, Malachi, because I was worrying about today and what I was going to say to Leah,' Esther murmured.

'The least said the better. As soon as she is well enough Tobiah and I will get her settled in some other village.'

'Oh Malachi, why, after all these years, did she come back?'

'I've told you why. She needed a place of refuge and she wanted to see Judith. She loved her sister.'

'I also thought she loved her mother and father. I have never understood her refusal to return to their home when she ran away from her husband. I can't believe she still won't see Ahava, when it must be obvious to her she is nearing the end of her days.'

'Well she isn't prepared to.' Malachi said sharply. 'And I don't want you stirring up trouble by questioning her about it. Leave well alone. Are you listening to me, Esther?'

Startled and wounded by the severity of his tone she stopped in her tracks and stared at him.

'I'm sorry,' he said, kissing her cheek. 'I shouldn't have spoke so harshly. It has been a difficult time. And like you I am worried about Ahava.'

She clutched at his arm, her hand shaking. 'I understand. Malachi. You can trust me. I promise I won't say a word to Leah about her mother.'

He nodded and his face took on a brooding look. 'It sits uneasily with me, keeping from Ahava the news that her daughter didn't die in that fire and that she is back in Sychar.'

Esther sighed loudly and slipped her hand in his holding it tight. They had reached the bottom of the olive grove before he spoke again.

'I have something to tell you that may cheer you. Simeon and his merchant friend will be passing through Sychar in a few weeks. Tobiah and I met them when we were on our way to bury Leah's son. They plan to break their homeward journey and take lodgings for the night in Tobiah's barn. So we might be able to buy some linen from them, at a good price, to make the wedding garments for when our daughter and Tobiah marry.'

Immediately Esther's spirits lifted and she beamed with excitement.

'That would be wonderful. I can hardly believe all this is really happening. Miriam is so happy.'

'I think her mother is happy too,' he said with a smile. 'We will have the first ceremony to mark their betrothal immediately following the celebration of Passover on Mount Gerizim. I am looking forward to hearing what Ahava will have to say when we tell her the news.'

He glanced sideways at his wife, his eyes glinting with amusement. Esther returned his look and he caught her arm, bringing her to a halt and holding her by her shoulders as he searched her face.

'You know it isn't easy to keep secrets in the village, Esther. People have sharp eyes and ears. Tobiah may have been seen when he brought Leah to his home or Miriam may let something slip.'

Esther stiffened with indignation.

'No Malachi, Miriam will not let anything slip. Our daughter is utterly trustworthy.'

He gave her a half smile in acknowledgement.

'I know that Esther. But right now her head is full of excitement about her betrothal to Tobiah. She may be indiscreet without realising it. Although Leah is certain the centurion intended her to go free there will always be those ready to betray us, for a shekel or two, if the authorities come asking questions,' he said grimly.

Esther pursed her lips and was about to praise the virtues and dependability of their daughter when Malachi, oblivious to her displeasure, began to walk on. She had to run to catch up in order to hear what he was saying.

'Fortunately we are going to be busy with the harvest. All the women from the village, except the old ones and those with babies, will be out helping. So there won't be time for any of them to be standing gossiping at the well and spreading rumours.' He pursed his lips as a thought occurred. 'Perhaps when Simeon comes we can arrange for him to take Leah with him across the Jordan, and settle her in Gerasa. There is money enough in that ring and those bangles to persuade him.'

'How much do you think they are worth,' Esther asked curiously.

'I really don't know. A lot. I have never seen such things in my life. But we must hurry now. Tobiah will be waiting for us.'

In the living room of his house Tobiah was standing by the table when he became aware of a presence behind him and he swung round to face Leah. As their eyes met he had the strange, disquieting sensation that he knew her, and that had known her for a long time. Yet that was not possible. She didn't look away and he was the first to drop his eyes. Disturbed, he gestured towards a jug of milk.

'Will you have some? It was brought fresh this morning.'

She nodded and sat down as he poured out a cupful. Carefully he avoided looking at her as he pushed a plate of bread and cheese towards her.

'Yesterday Malachi and I went back to the place where I found you. We went to recover the body of your son.'

Leah took a sharp gasp of breath and clenched her fists.

'We wrapped him in linen cloths and took him to the tomb belonging to my family,' he said, more gently.

Beyond words she stared at him, her breathing shallow and harsh. She was totally unprepared for such kindness. The deep, raging pain that she had been struggling to control since Marcellus murdered Daniel, welled and broke in a torrent of tears. Carefully Tobiah sat down by her side. This was an agony he understood and he waited, a silent comforting presence, until finally she stopped, exhausted. He soaked a cloth in water and handed it to her and she pressed it to her face.

In a flurry of movement the dog jumped up from the mat where it had been sleeping and raced, with a high-pitched bark, towards the door, skidding in excitement as it shot through. Relieved by the interruption Tobiah went to the window and looked out across the courtyard. When he turned back to Leah he was struck again by the elusive feeling of recognition.

'It's Malachi,' he said softly. 'We will be out working in the fields until sundown. Esther is with him. She will stay with you today. She is skilled at making medicines and she will be able to help heal your injuries.

With her composure regained, Leah stood to face him. 'I know you must be worried that the Roman authorities will come looking for me. They won't. I'm sure the centurion intended me to go free, and that no harm will come to you or the village because of me. But as soon as I'm able I shall leave your home, she said firmly.'

To his bewilderment he knew that he didn't want her to go. Thrown into turmoil, by uncomfortable emotions he couldn't understand, he remained looking at her helplessly, until Esther came bustling into the room. Her face was wreathed in smiles as she greeted him.

'Malachi is waiting for you, Tobiah, and the hired labourers are already in the fields.'

Relieved by the interruption he was out through the door almost before she had finished speaking and the two women were left facing each other.

With the disappearance of Tobiah the smile on Esther's face faded. She gave Leah a hostile stare; her innate compassion buried beneath her fear for what trouble might lie in this woman's wake.

'So, you have come back to us,' she said, fighting down the urge to take her in her arms.

Leah opened her mouth to answer and she held up her hand.

'No, don't say anything. Let me tell you what is going to happen. You must take the medicine I have brought and use the ointment on your bruises. And you are to remain inside the house until Malachi and Tobiah can make arrangements for you to settle in some other village.'

She paused, struggling with the tremble in her voice that she was finding hard to control. She turned her head so that she wasn't looking at Leah.

'Malachi tells me you have no intention of telling Tobiah that you are his mother. Under the circumstances I think it's for the best. He and Miriam are to marry and I don't want you upsetting him.'

As she spoke Leah's eyes darkened with pain. This was the woman who had wrapped her arms around her in comfort so many times when she had been a child, and who now had not one consoling word to say about what had befallen her. She felt bereft.

Mustering her courage Esther turned to look at her again and she was shocked by the expression of despair on Leah's face. Yet still she could not afford to allow pity to deflect her, because there was Miriam to consider.

Leah gave a short, hoarse laugh that ended on a sob.

'How you have changed Esther. I would never have thought that you, of all people, could become so hard.'

'I don't know how you dare say that to me Leah. There is no one harder or more selfish than you.'

Tears spilled onto her cheeks and she dashed them away. She felt as though her legs could no longer hold her and it took all her willpower to remain standing and say what was on her mind, before her courage failed.

'After you ran away from your husband, and Malachi arranged for you to go to Caesarea with Mary and Samuel, were you grateful? No you were not. Only a few months later it appears you left their home and the work they provided for you. Then you had a child by a man you are not prepared to talk about and ended up being sold as a slave. I dread to think what trouble might be following you.' Her breathing became laboured. 'Why won't you see your mother?'

The words had tumbled from her mouth before she could help herself. She gave a short gasp and put her fingers on her lips.

'That has nothing to do with you,' Leah said softly.

With the back of her hand Esther wiped her forehead, the flush on her face deepening. She was unused to quarrelling and she didn't know how to put it right.

'I must congratulate you, Esther, on your daughter's betrothal to Tobiah,' Leah said, ignoring the pleading look that Esther was giving her. 'Miriam has done well for herself. I am sure she will make certain everything goes according to her plans.'

There was something in her tone, and what she had said, that confused Esther and she began to stammer.

'I don't know what you mean. Are you implying that Miriam has somehow trapped Tobiah?'

Coolly, Leah smiled and Esther fidgeted uncomfortably with the sash around her waist.

'How could I be implying any such thing? I only met your daughter for the first time yesterday.'

Turning her back on Leah, Esther picked up her bag of herbs and ointments, making a clattering noise as she banged it down on the table.

'Tobiah has been widowed for over a year now. It's time for him to be thinking of marrying again and it is my daughter he has chosen,' she said defensively, as she faced her again. 'Go and lie down, Leah, you look dreadful. I'll make up a drink that will help you sleep.'

Her hands shook as she removed the small pots from her bag and she wanted to cry. She was an uncomplicated, loving woman, neither ungenerous nor unkind and yet she had been both to Leah. Now she was struggling with feelings of guilt and shame that were unfamiliar to her.

Impulsively Leah crossed to her side, catching hold of her arm and pulling her round so that they were facing each other.

'You were always kind to me as a child Esther. You and Malachi. I have never forgotten that. Nor have I forgotten how close you and my sister were. You must miss her deeply. Please believe that I only want Tobiah's happiness.'

'That is what we all want Leah, and he seems to have found it with my daughter. I promise you, wherever you go next you can be sure of one thing, Tobiah will have a good and obedient wife in Miriam and she will look after him well.'

Leah clamped her mouth shut, her face darkening with suppressed fury at what she had overheard between Miriam and the goat herder the previous day, when they thought she was sleeping. Esther drew back, startled by her expression. Before anything further could be said Miriam burst through the doorway gasping for breath, her face suffused with excitement. She thumped the water jar she was carrying onto the floor, slopping its contents. Shocked into action Esther flew to her daughter's side and grabbed her arm.

'What is it?' she screamed.

Miriam's breathing came in deep shuddering gasps and she was almost incoherent as she struggled to speak.

'Stop!' Leah said firmly. 'Take a deep breath, Miriam, and start again, slowly.'

Esther stared, open mouthed, at her daughter and her body began to shake, uncontrollably.

'Mother, there's a Roman centurion...' she paused dramatically and flung out an arm towards Leah. 'Asking about her.'

The blood drained from Esther's face and with her legs no longer able to support her she slid to the floor. Leah crossed quickly to her side and hauled her up in a tight grip.

'Listen to me Esther, I know this man. He will not want to harm anyone who has helped me. Get a stool for your mother, Miriam.'

Jolted into action by the pallor of her mother's face and the sharpness of Leah's tone, Miriam dragged a stool forward. Esther sank down onto it twisting her hands in her lap.

'How can you be so sure Leah?' she said, anger hardening her voice as the colour returned to her face. 'You are an escaped slave and I doubt that the ring and bangles, that Malachi told me you have, belong to you. Not only will he want to take you back to the city and have you tried by the authorities as runaway slave and thief, he will want anyone who has helped you punished too.'

Miriam stared at her mother, rigid with shock at what she had just heard. As she digested the implications, her face twisted into an ugly grimace and she pointed a finger at Leah.

'What are you going to do about this?' she hissed through clenched teeth.

Shocked by the venom in her tone, and Esther's accusation that she was a thief, Leah faltered, then a thick wave of anger swept over her. More roughly than she intended she grabbed Miriam by her arm and dragged her closer. The girl's eyes widened in alarm.

'Where was the centurion when he spoke to you?'

'At the bottom of the village, on the path leading to Jacob's well. He had tethered his horse to a tree and was sitting on the ground.'

'Was there anyone else around?'

'No.'

'What did he say, exactly?'

'Let go of my arm and I'll tell you.' With her courage returning she glared at Leah. 'He asked if a woman of your description had recently come to live in the village and I pretended that I was deaf and unable to speak.'

Leah smiled coldly, promising herself she would never underestimate this girl.

'Go back quickly and tell him that I will meet him at the well at noon.'

Miriam hesitated, looking from Leah to her mother. 'Suppose he thinks I should be punished for not telling him straight away that I knew where you were,' she muttered, her eyes widening with fear.

'He will have no interest in you, or in punishing you. He will know you were frightened,' Leah said abruptly.

Their eyes locked and it was Miriam who looked away first. Esther heaved herself from the stool, scrubbing away the tears from her face with the palms of her hands.

'Miriam is having nothing more to do with this,' she sad flatly.

Leah tucked an escaped strand of hair back under her veil and her voice was low and urgent.

'Listen to me Esther. It is better he leaves now, before anyone else sees him, and that I meet him at the well when it is deserted. If he decides to search the village and finds me in Tobiah's home Ahava would never let it rest until she had the whole story.'

There was a bleak emptiness in her eyes as they met and held Esther's.

'I don't think he has come to take me back to Sebaste as a recaptured slave. But if I'm wrong you would be rid of me, and no one would be any the wiser.'

Esther struggled against the desire to take Leah in her arms and hold her. 'Why should he believe you will keep your word to meet him at the well? He might force Miriam to bring him here and have us all arrested.'

'He won't. I know him. He will trust me to be there. And Miriam will be in no danger from him.'

Esther stared at her breathing deeply. Abruptly she appeared to make up her mind. 'Go now, Miriam. Give him the message and return immediately,' she said.

Miriam frowned, about to argue.

'Go,' Esther shouted, pushing her towards the door.

After Miriam left the two women sat in silence neither one feeling that they had anything more to say to the other.

Chapter Fourteen

When Miriam reached the point on the path where she had last seen the centurion he was still sitting beneath the tree, his helmet on the ground beside him. She stopped, just out of sight and smoothed down her tunic, pulling the sash around her waist tighter and biting her lips until they reddened. With a gentle sway of her hips and a soft smile she walked towards him, her eyes boldly meeting and holding his.

He watched her, his face expressionless, as he bit down hard into the apple he was holding. Her smile widened and with a delicate downward movement of her head she shifted her gaze, only to quickly glance up at him again from under her lashes.

The apple dropped from his hand and in a quick, fluid movement he lifted himself from the ground to stand towering over her. His physical presence and the strong smell of leather and horse that clung to him excited her and she thought she saw him give a fleeting smile.

'So, girl, I thought you might return. Have you managed to find your voice whilst you've been gone?' He threw back his head and laughed, his eyes crinkling at the corners with amusement, and her heartbeat quickened.

'I'm sorry,' she murmured as she moved back a step. 'I was afraid.'

Feeling surer of herself now, she lowered her head submissively whilst she calculated how she could turn this encounter to her advantage. The silence lengthened until she heard his voice coming from a distance.

'What's your name girl?'

She looked up, shocked to find that he was sitting astride his horse. The sun was reflecting off his helmet and catching its red plumed crest as it stirred in the breeze

'What is your name girl?' he repeated, louder this time.

'Miriam,' she answered quickly, looking up at him with more courage than she was feeling.

'Well, Miriam, now that you have found your tongue is there something you have come back to tell me?'

His voice had a cold, hard edge and despite her outward show of boldness she began to tremble. The horse tossed its head and took a couple of prancing steps towards her. He leaned forward in the saddle and put a calming hand on its neck.

'Come on, girl, speak up,'

Her confidence had deserted her and she began to tremble. 'I am to tell you that the woman you are looking for will meet you at noon at Jacob's well,' she said, carefully spacing out each word to control the shaking of her voice.

As she backed away he moved around, until the sun was behind him. The shadow of horse and rider spread across her and her heart started to race. Before she could move he had seized her arm and pulled her to him. She could feel the hardness of his calf against her breast and the heat coming from the horse. His grip tightened and she clenched her teeth, determined not to let him see her fear as she stared up at him.

'You're hurting me.'

He dropped her arm, and she stumbled backwards, almost falling. As she recovered her balance she turned to run. Swiftly he manoeuvred his horse blocking her escape. She stared up at him, her eyes wide with fear, all coquettishness gone.

'What are you going to do to me?' she stammered.

'I'm not going to do anything to you,' he said after a long pause. 'But just think for a moment, girl, what I could do if I were so minded. I am sure you have the imagination.' Amused, he laughed out loud.

With a struggle she managed to control the rising tide of fear that was threatening to engulf her. She rearranged her features into a sulky pout and stamped her foot hard on the ground. He threw back his head and laughed again. Immediately she regretted what she had done. It had been childish and she did not want to appear childish before this man.

'If nothing else you have nerve,' he said. Then he stopped laughing and his expression hardened.

'I think your father should have given you a beating long ago. Has he not warned you how dangerous it is to play the harlot? Be thankful that it's me and not some other soldier you have tried your tricks on today.'

There was such cold contempt in his voice that she gasped for breath. Her face flushed as tears of anger and humiliation began to run down her cheeks.

'Tell Leah I will be waiting for her,' he said as he rode off.

Two hours later Leah set out for Jacob's well, carrying a large water pitcher. She stooped deliberately and her veil was pulled low on her forehead and covering the lower half of her face. From a distance she could be mistaken for any of the elderly women from the village. If anyone out in the fields were to notice her they would not be curious, just surprised she was out walking at that time of day.

Deep in thought she felt neither the intense heat of the sun nor the hot, stony track that was scorching her feet through the soles of her sandals. As she neared the well she stopped and shaded her eyes with her hand. In the distance she could see the figure of a Roman soldier on horseback, and a sob caught in her throat as an overwhelming sense of despair and loss swept over her.

She lowered the pitcher to the ground and breathed deeply as she tried to calm her thoughts. She wondered why he had come for her. She knew that as a Roman officer he was duty bound to take her back to the city and have her tried as a runaway slave. Yet when he pressed the emerald ring into her hand she had believed he was offering her freedom.

During the three years she had been Marcellus's concubine he had often spoken to her of Varinius. He had told her of his reputation for bravery and honour and how he was idolised by the soldiers under his command. She knew also, that despite his love for Marcellus, he had often berated him angrily about his brutality towards her. He was a good man, neither cruel nor mean-spirited, and she consoled herself with the thought that he would not bring harm those who had sheltered her.

The heat felt oppressive and the wound on her head throbbed with pain. She watched him trot his horse towards her until he was close enough for her to feel the hot breath billowing from its nostrils and she felt herself sway. He dismounted quickly and passed her his water skin and she drank greedily until he took it gently from her.

'A little at a time Leah, a little at a time,' he said laughing.

With her eyes fixed on his she wiped her mouth with the back of her hand and straightened her shoulders.

'I've come as I promised, Varinius, and I am ready to return to Sebaste with you. But I beg you, please, don't punish those in the village who have helped me. They are good people. Let it be enough that you have found me.'

He smiled and his voice was gentle. 'I don't want to punish anyone Leah, least of all you. But I do want you to come with me,' he said, moving closer until they were within inches of each other.

'Are you taking me back to Sebaste?'

Without answering he put his hands around her waist and lifted her onto his horse. Hot, angry tears welled as she thought of the pointless sacrifice Daniel had made in helping her escape, and the wild idea of gathering up the reins and riding off raced through her mind. Before the thought could take hold his foot was in the stirrup and he was up in the saddle behind her, holding her firmly with one hand and guiding the horse forward with the other.

It was a while before she became aware that he had turned the horse north, not west towards Sebaste, and that they were riding across the open plain. They dropped down into a valley and rode for half a mile, before climbing again and heading towards a grove of ancient olive trees that were fringing the lower slopes of the hills. Reining in his horse he lifted her from the saddle and took her by her arm, leading her into the trees. Confused she struggled to free herself. He stopped and looked down at her his expression solemn.

'There is no need to be afraid Leah. I only want to talk to you. In the shade of the trees we will be sheltered from the heat.'

He shrugged off his cloak and spread it on the ground, laying his helmet on top. Then he signalled her to sit beside to him. The sun, slanting through the branches, made patterns of light on their faces and neither of them felt in any hurry to break the strange, dreamlike unreality of the moment. It was Varinius who spoke first, quietly saying her name. She turned her head and looked at him. With a gentle finger he stroked the bruising on her arm and his eyes were infinitely sad.

'I am sorry for Daniel's murder and the way in which you have suffered. I am sorry too for the way I had to leave you both.'

'I just wish I could have died with my son,' she said, and she was surprised by her calmness.

He put an arm around her and she didn't resist as he pulled her closer to him, allowing her to rest her head against his shoulder.

'I went back yesterday, late in the afternoon, to where I had left you, hoping you would still be alive. When I discovered that both you and Daniel's body had gone, I suspected it must have been someone from Sychar who had given you shelter and taken your son to a burial ground.'

Her body stiffened and she lifted her head from his shoulder.

'I was helped. But please, don't try to find out who it was and have them punished.'

'I have told you, Leah, I have no intention of doing that. There has been more than enough violence and pain.'

He reached behind his breastplate and brought out a purse, heavy with money, holding it out towards her.

'I came to give you this. And there is something I need to tell you.' He looked down at the purse, weighing it in his hands.

Bewildered, she stared at him as he dropped it into her lap. 'I don't understand. Why would you want to give me money? You know I have the ring and the bracelets.'

'Yes I do,' he said patiently. But money will be more useful, and safer than trying to barter a ring and gold bracelets that someone may suspect you have stolen. Or may try to steal from you.' He stared past her into the distance.

'You said you had something you wanted to tell me,' Varinius.'

The silence lengthened and he sighed before he spoke. 'I know you and Marcellus were married,' he said softly. 'I found the papers when I was sorting out his affairs. So, you were not a slave when you ran away, you were his wife. What I have to tell you is that the marriage is not legally valid in the eyes of Rome because you are not a Roman citizen. I'm sorry Leah, his father will make sure that you don't inherit his fortune.'

She shook her head in disbelief. 'Marcellus was wildly drunk when he forced me into that marriage. He was laughing later when he told me that it was just another of his charades.'

'No, it wasn't. You and he were married.'

For a moment she couldn't speak, then she gave a harsh, bitter laugh. 'The bracelets and the ring rightfully belong to me and I bear the scars that purchased them. I want nothing else from him.'

'I though you might say that.'

Frowning she held up the purse. 'Is this your money, Varinius, or is it Marcellus's money?'

'It is my money.'

Her mind was in turmoil. 'What is it you want from me?'

'I would like to tell you a little about the Marcellus I grew up with, if you would allow me to,' he said haltingly. 'I know the harm he did you and the harm he did others too, and it was inexcusable. But he wasn't always the brutal, depraved man you came to fear and despise.

'He knew what he had become and that knowledge was destroying him. It was as though the Marcellus I had known and loved since I was a boy no longer existed. But I will understand if you don't want to hear what I have to say. The money is not a bribe.'

She suffered a wrenching confusion of disbelief and anger that he could think she would want to hear anything good he had to say about the man who had murdered her son and she tried to stand. Gently he caught her wrist and pulled her back down.

'I'm sorry Leah. It was wrong of me. Please forget what I said.'

The look of pain in his eyes wounded her and she wanted to hold and comfort him. But she couldn't. Instead she remained sitting stiffly by his side, her hands clenched in her lap. In the strained silence that settled between them she tried to close her mind to what he had asked and the fury that it had awakened in her.

She could hear his breathing and feel the tension in his body and slowly the anger began to drain from her. He too was suffering from the grief of losing someone he had loved and she felt a stirring of pity. He needed to remember the boy and man Marcellus had been, before his demons claimed him, and share those memories.'

'All right, Varinius, I'm listening,' she said softly.

He took her hand in his and she watched the expressions flitting across his face as his thoughts took shape. When he finally spoke his voice was hesitant, almost as though he didn't know where to begin.

'When Marcellus was a boy he was always very studious, but he was also funny, gentle and kind. And as a young man his friends knew they could always depend on him, because he had a reputation then for being honourable and reliable. He was generous too, both with his time and his money. And he was clever, Leah. The Greek philosophers were his passion and he could debate their ideas with the best. His head was always in a book and he wrote the most beautiful poetry.'

'I sometimes saw a little of that man,' she said thoughtfully. 'When he was not the worse for drink, and his demons were at bay, he would talk to me for hours about many things. I learned a great deal from him then. I learned to think.'

A smile lit up Varinius face and for a moment the shadows lifted. She saw how much he had been moved and comforted by what she had said and she wanted him to be comforted.

'When the mood was upon him he had endless patience with me. Especially when he talked about the philosophers and their ideas. If there were things I didn't understand he would explain them carefully until I did. I even grew to like him a little then, until he changed again into the brutal man I had come to fear.'

Varinius's eyes had taken on a far away look and she knew, from his expression, that he was somewhere in the past with Marcellus. After a while he gave a long, drawn out sigh.

'He became sick in his mind Leah. I watched it develop slowly over many years and once it took hold he pushed away everyone who tried to help him, including me. I know that he loved you and longed for you to love him, but then he behaved in a way towards you that could have only have made you hate him. Although I believe he hated himself more.'

His eyes clouded with pain and impulsively she took him in her arms and drew his head onto her breast, stroking him like a child.

'How did it happen, Varinius? What caused the change in him?'

He pulled free and shook his head, small lines appearing at the corners of his eyes as he screwed them tight in thought.

'I think the damage occurred when he was very young. His father is extremely wealthy and he used that wealth to control Marcellus. He is also an ambitious man, hungry for the political power he never achieved for himself, but hoped his son might achieve for him.

'It was always his intention that Marcellus should be a career soldier and his aspirations were for him to become legate of a legion. He wanted him to reach the highest position in the army that would advance a political career in the Senate when he retired. He thought the way to achieve that ambition was to treat Marcellus roughly from being a child. He beat him severely and often, even for the most minor of things, and belittled and undermined every one of his achievements. He believed it would spur him on to greater effort. Never once did he praise him for any of his accomplishments.

'When Marcellus joined the army at twenty-three it was with the rank of tribune because of his families equestrian status, and he excelled in the role. Four years later he was promoted on his own merit. But there was no word of congratulations or praise from his father.

'Over the next few years he began to change, then things started to go badly wrong. It was as though he had given up. He was no longer able to believe in his own worth and he began to despise himself. I think all the violence and coarseness that grew in him were manifestations of his despair that no matter what he achieved he could never win his father's love or approval.'

After he finished speaking they sat in silence for a long while until he became aware that she was crying. He lifted her chin and wiped away the tears with his fingers and she shook her head and tried to smile.

'I am not crying for Marcellus, I am crying for a little girl I once knew,' she said. The words caught in her throat and her face betrayed the vulnerability that she always tried to keep hidden from the world.

'Was that little girl you, Leah?'

She looked away neither denying nor an admitting what he had asked and when she turned to him again there was no trace of weakness in her expression. Varinius watched her carefully for a while before he spoke.

'I would like to tell you about another man, Leah, if you will allow me,' he said.

Mystified and too emotionally drained to refuse she nodded her head.

'Three months ago, whilst I was travelling through Judea, I came across a Galilean rabbi named Jesus. There was a large crowd around him, and I stopped to listen to what he was saying. He is the most extraordinary teacher and healer,' he said, keeping his eyes fixed on a point in the distance.

She looked at him in astonishment and for a moment she was about to tell him, coldly, that she was a Samaritan woman and a Jewish rabbi was of no interest to her. Then she caught the expression on his face.

'Go on,' she said, softly.

'I have long been an admirer of Judaism, Leah. The morality enshrined in the Ten Commandments and the unshakeable belief of Jews in the one God, has the respect of many of my countrymen. Yet even though I have often wished to convert fully to the faith, I feel unable to do so. The dietary laws and the detailed commands of the Torah are too daunting, particularly circumcision,' he said, with a wry smile.

'But Jesus is teaching wholly new things about people and their relationship with God, and with each other. Things that are overwhelming, liberating and inclusive. His deepest concern is for what lies in the heart of a person not how well they perform their religious duties.'

He took her hand in his and his eyes were bright with fervour.

'The army brutalises men Leah, until we stop seeing the human being in those whose lands we invade. But Jesus did not condemn me for being a soldier or for my allegiance to Rome and to Caesar. He knew that I had no alternative other than to continue in the army until my discharge. But what I do have control over is how I behave towards the soldiers under my command and the people whose countries we conquer and occupy, and those we take into slavery. I wish you could meet and talk with him.'

She removed her hand and her laugh had a hollow, bitter ring. 'You know as well I, Varinius, no Jewish rabbi would be seen with a Samaritan. Jews despise us. They believe we're an inferior race. But that aside, no rabbi, Jewish or Samaritan, would consider a woman capable of understanding religious teaching.'

'Look at me,' he said, taking her chin in his hand. 'This man would. His message about God's love, compassion and mercy is for everyone: man or woman, Jew or Gentile. He knew everything about me, Leah, and yet still he said I was precious in the sight of God. I intend now to follow his teaching.'

Gently he reached out and stroked the scar on her face, his expression thoughtful.

'Who was Daniel's father?'

'He was a Jew. When he chose to marry me he didn't know I was a Samaritan. And I saw no reason to enlighten him. He is dead now.'

Although there was a closed look on her face, that discouraged any further discussion about her former husband, the atmosphere between them was not uncomfortable.

'I might like to hear this rabbi preach,' she said cautiously.

'I hope one day you will. His teaching has transformed my life.'

He stood and held out a hand, pulling her up and holding her by her shoulders.

'I loved Marcellus, but I hated what he had become. It comforts me that you saw a little of the goodness that was in him. But I know it is too much to ask that you forgive him all the harm he has done you.'

She met his eyes and they were filled with a pleading that belied his words.

'Perhaps if he had not murdered my son I may have been able to forgive him for what he did to me.' She shook her head and her voice hardened. 'But I will never forgive him for that.'

'I am sorry, Leah. The grief of a mother for her child who has been murdered must be truly terrible.' There was sadness in his eyes as he looked at her. 'I suspected a long time ago that Daniel was your son, the likeness was there'

'And yet you never told Marcellus.'

'No. I wasn't able to protect you from his brutality but I thought I could protect Daniel by keeping your secret. In the end I wasn't able to do that either. I hope in time, Leah, you will be able to find some comfort and peace in the happier memories you have of your son.'

He pulled her towards him and she rested her head on his chest, listening the slow, even beat of his heart. And in the warmth of the silence that flowed between them his breathing rose and fell with hers. After a while he released her and bent to retrieve his cloak and helmet from the ground.

'It is unlikely that we shall meet again. At the end of next month my posting here comes to an end and I shall be going to Rome to visit with Marcellus's father. Afterwards I will be rejoining my legion in Syria. Use the money wisely, Leah. Come, I will take you back as far as Jacob's well.'

Chapter Fifteen

Leah arrived back at Tobiah's house to find it deserted. The only sound on the still afternoon air was the clucking of hens, as they scratched and pecked at the crumbs that had fallen from the bread oven by the door. She hesitated on the threshold and took a deep breath before entering.

Cautiously she made her way to the bedroom, where she pushed the purse of money beneath the mattress, to lie with the ring and bangles. With a feeling of utter exhaustion, and with every bone in her body aching she lay down. Her last thoughts before sleep claimed her were of Daniel.

It was dark when she awoke and she could hear noises coming from the next room. Rising from the mattress she crossed the floor to stand framed in the doorway. Tobiah was lifting the lid from a steaming cooking pot. As he became aware of her he smiled and she sensed the change in him. Although there were lines of tiredness around his eyes the strain had disappeared from his face and he appeared relaxed and cheerful.

'Good, you are awake,' he said. 'Come and have something to eat. Esther has made more than enough for both of us.'

She hesitated, then walked to the table and sat down. She had not eaten since early that morning, but still she had no appetite, and the smell of the stew made her feel nauseous. As she picked at the food that Tobiah had ladled into her bowl she could feel him watching her.

'Esther sent Miriam to the fields to tell me that the centurion had come looking for you and that you had gone to meet him at Jacob's well,' he said.

'Yes, I did, but don't be alarmed. It is not his intention to have anyone who helped me arrested. Nor had he come to take me back to Sebaste.'

Tobiah nodded and laughed softly. 'I know. You would not be here now if he had. As soon as I realised you had returned I went straight down to the village and told Malachi and Esther. They will sleep easier tonight.' He cleared his throat. 'What did he come for?'

She frowned and began shredding the piece of bread she had been eating and the question hung in the air between them. He placed a hand over hers and stilled her fingers.

'It doesn't matter; you don't need to tell me. The important thing is that he has gone and will not be coming back.'

Preoccupied by the thoughts his question had raised she nodded, vaguely. As she became aware that he was repeating her name she struggled to focus her mind.

'I'm sorry,' she said. 'Were you saying something?'

Stung by the flatness and lack of interest in her voice he spoke more brusquely than he intended.

'You must be aware, Leah, that it isn't possible for you to remain in my home for much longer, without someone discovering who you are.

'Yes, I am. Please don't worry, I will...'

Ashamed, he stopped her before she could finish speaking. 'Forgive me, I didn't mean to sound harsh. You are my aunt and I want to help you. Now we are no longer in danger from the authorities, I thought if you made your peace with my grandmother you could both live together in her house.'

He saw something shift and harden in her eyes. Unsure of himself he began tapping his fingers on the table in a nervous beat. Leah clasped her hands tightly in her lap and turned her head. If she had not felt so touched by the sincerity of his proposal, she would have laughed, because she would never consider living in her mother's home.

When she turned to look at him again the hardness in her eyes had been replaced with sadness, and he was struck again by the strange sensation that he knew her, and that he had known her for a long time. He was aware that he was staring and he couldn't look away. Shockingly he felt that he wanted to reach out and touch her, and that somehow he already knew the feel of her arms around him.

'You and Malachi have done more than enough for me already, she said gently, breaking into his thoughts. 'It is better that I leave. If Daniel had lived we would not have remained in Sychar.'

She took a deep, shuddering breath as the tearing anger and guilt at his death rose in her breast, almost overwhelming her. He waited patiently, ready to convince her, when she calmed, of the good sense of his proposal. As the raw pain subsided, and her breathing steadied, she prepared herself for the hurt she was about to inflict, knowing that she would destroy forever the fragile threads of something precious growing between them. And she wished again that she had died with Daniel.

'I can't live with my mother, Tobiah. Nor can I stay in here. I have lived too long as the concubine of an important man in the comfort and sophistication of a wealthy Roman home. I need to be in the civilised surroundings of a city with its shops, libraries and theatres, not stuck in the middle of the country with goats and sheep.'

She watched as his expression turned from disbelief to dark anger and the hurt in his eyes brought the sting of tears to hers.

'Do you also want to be with another man who would beat you half to death?' He said, his voice tight with suppressed fury. 'Tell me Leah where are you going to find the money to set yourself up in such a manner?'

'You know I have a valuable ring and bracelets, and I also have a purse of money that the centurion has given me.'

He stared at her in astonishment as he struggled to make sense of what she had just said.

'Why did he give you money? What did he want from you?' he asked sharply.

'He wanted to talk about Marcellus and for me to forgive him. And he gave me the money out of the goodness of his heart.'

Tobiah's face flushed dark with anger. 'You are refusing to make peace with your own mother, so tell me, how do you think you are going to be able to forgive the man who murdered your son?'

'I don't know.'

She closed her eyes and he knew that she was no longer aware of him or of her surroundings. Unable to reach out to her he stared down at his hands, clasped in his lap, the knuckles showing white. After a while she opened her eyes and touched him gently on his arm.

'What I do know, Tobiah, is that I owe it to Daniel to go on living. But in living I will have to endure each day the pain of his death and the guilt I feel for allowing him to help me escape. And then there is the hatred that burns in me for Marcellus. Guilt and hatred are terrible burdens. The weight of them, and the energy needed to sustain them, destroys as surely as a sword through the heart. If I cannot find a way to forgive Marcellus, and myself, every memory I have of Daniel will be tainted and overshadowed by those feelings, until the beauty that was my son is buried beneath them.'

He took her hands in his. 'Wouldn't forgiving the Roman be a betrayal of Daniel?'

'Perhaps the greater betrayal would be to allow the guilt and the hatred to destroy me. Because then Daniel's death will have been for nothing.'

'I think I understand something of what you are saying. When my wife and my newborn son died I was consumed by a terrible rage. It was too soon for him to come into the world and Rebekah was not strong enough to survive his birth. Then four days ago I held the child of her sister in my arms and the rage left me. As I looked down on that baby I knew I should try to be grateful for each day and live it well in memory of my wife and son.' A puzzled frown crossed his face. 'I don't know who it was I was so angry with.'

'Perhaps it was Rebekah and your son, for having died and left you. And yourself too, because you were not able to save them.'

She held him in her strange, mesmerising gaze. 'The centurion told me about someone today.' She paused as one of the oil lamps flickered and went out, and the moment slipped away.

He let go of her hands and stood with his back towards her. She could hear him breathing and when he turned to face her again his fists were clenched at his sides and her heart began to race.

'What is it that Malachi knows about you that he is so afraid of me finding out?'

She stared at him and he saw the panic in her eyes.

'He knows nothing other than what you know yourself,' she said, her voice tripping on the lie.

The dog had appeared at his side and he bent to stroke it. When he straightened there was a look of such intensity in his face that it frightened her, and she held her breath. He picked up a rolled mattress and walked towards the doorway, then stopped and turned to face her again.

'I don't believe you. Nor do I believe the reasons you have given me for wanting to leave Sychar.'

He held her eyes, and she couldn't look away.

'But might I ask, whilst you are in the mood for forgiving that you extend that forgiveness to my grandmother for whatever wrong you feel she has done you. It surely cannot be any worse than what the Roman did.'

She gasped and he raised his hand.

'Don't say anything now but please, consider what I have asked. I will be out in the fields again all day tomorrow and so will most of the village. Miriam will be helping my grandmother with the milling and I have told Malachi that you have no need of Esther.'

Without looking at her he left the house and climbed the stairs to the roof, where, for long into the night, he lay awake, shifting restlessly as his mind teemed with thoughts of all that had happened.

Chapter Sixteen

For most of the night Leah too lay awake, her eyes wide open and sightless, her senses mercifully numbed as her mind shut down, protecting her from a grief too great to bear. Nothing intruded. There was only a blessed emptiness, until the pale light of dawn pushed through the opening in the window shutters, and then she slept.

When she awoke the room felt hot and airless. She lay on her back for a while, before slowly stretching her limbs and getting up from the mattress. Calmly and unhurriedly she removed her clothes until she stood naked. With her head tilted to one side she listened for any noise that might indicate the presence of someone else in the house. When all remained quiet she picked up an empty water pitcher and walked outside, to stand blinking in the bright light of the mid-morning sun.

With slow, careful steps she made her way to the cistern at the back of the house where she began to wash; pouring water over her head until it ran in streams down her body, droplets clinging to her and reflecting the sun's rays in myriad pricks of light.

She stood perfectly still watching the two donkeys grazing in the field. One of them looked up to stare at her. With a graceful movement of her neck she bent her head and swept her hair forward, twisting it into a coil and squeezing until it ceased to drip. Her eyes closed and she lifted her face to the sun, feeling the water evaporate from her skin as her body dried.

Without hurrying she retraced her steps into the house and dressed. She wasn't hungry but she prepared a bowl of corn porridge and sat down to eat, slowly swallowing every mouthful and drinking the remains of yesterday's milk, which was now turning sour. When she had finished she pushed her bowl away and walked outside again.

Languidly she wandered around the courtyard, coming to rest before the potter's wheel and running her hand across it. Tobiah's discarded clay pots lay stacked in an untidy heap on the ground. She lifted one and held it up in her hands without really seeing it. Then she put it down again in its exact place and made her way towards a wooden bench beneath the shade of a small palm tree. She sat down and folded her hands in her lap, waiting for the numbness to go and feeling to return.

Indistinctly at first, and then louder, she heard the sound of Caleb driving the goats through the olive grove towards the house to deliver the days milk. Her eyes snapped open. As he entered the courtyard he was humming softly, until he saw her, then he stopped, unsure of what to do.

'Come in, Caleb,' she said softly. 'Neither Tobiah nor Miriam are here, it is quite safe.'

His hand jerked and the milk spilled out of the jar. Then he lost his grip and it smashed to the ground. He was sure she must be able to hear the wild thumping of his heart as he stared down, horrified, at the broken pieces of clay and the spreading white puddle.

'Who are you?' he muttered, immediately regretting the insolence of his question. He looked down quickly at his feet.

She smiled. 'It doesn't matter who I am. What does matter is that I overheard you and Miriam in the house the other day. I know what you have both been doing and the plans you have been making to steal Tobiah's money after he and Miriam marry.'

Caleb's face drained of colour. Twice he tried to speak and twice his voice failed him.

'Sit down,' she commanded, indicating a place beside her on the bench.

He remained rooted to the spot. His legs were trembling so hard that they could no longer propel him forward, or hold him up, and he sank to the ground in front of her, dropping his chin onto his chest.

'Tell me,' her voice was kinder now. 'Do you really think that such a preposterous plan will work?'

Without looking up he shook his head.

'I don't know,' he mumbled. 'Miriam says…..'

'I'm not interested in what Miriam says. Tell me how you feel about it, Caleb.'

Mollified by the gentleness of her tone, he lifted his head and stared at her, not knowing how to begin.

She remained very still with her hands cupped in her lap, her body inclined slightly towards him. He frowned, his eyes shifting from side to side as he considered what to say. He had the strangest feeling he could tell her anything and that she would understand. She smiled and waited. In a rush of words he began to speak.

'I'm indebted to Tobiah and I have never wanted to do anything to harm him. It was all Miriam's idea. She said her father would never allow her to marry a penniless goat herder but that she had a plan.'

'I think it's cowardly to blame everything on Miriam. Don't you?'

He bit down hard on his bottom lip, drawing blood.

'Does it hurt you that Malachi would not want you as a husband for his daughter?' she asked softly.

Roughly he wiped the back of his hand across his lips, smearing the blood onto his chin.

'Yes, but I understand it. Why would he want someone as poor as I am, as a husband for her? She is beautiful; there will be many men who will want her as a wife.'

'You sound angry, Caleb.'

For a moment he looked startled, as though she had said something he couldn't understand, then he gave a bitter smile.

'I haven't really thought about it before but, yes, I suppose I am angry. Malachi might be Tobiah's steward and an important man in the village but he doesn't own land. And he works for Tobiah, just the same as I.'

'It feels as though you don't like him much.'

A deep frown furrowed his forehead as he chewed over her words and then he sighed.

'I do like Malachi and I am grateful to him. He has always been kind to me. Sometimes, when I've tethered the goats for the night, he will find me work sweeping out the carpentry shop belonging to his sons, so I can earn a little extra money.'

His voice broke and he angrily brushed away tears from his eyes. 'But he would never agree to Miriam marrying me; he wants someone better for her than a goat herder.'

'Do you want to marry her?'

'It doesn't matter whether I do or not, she's betrothed now to Tobiah.' With a sulky frown he dropped his head onto his chest again.

'Yes, she is. But neither of you are going to allow that to stand in your way, are you?'

His head jerked up. Her tone had been light but something lay beneath it that made him afraid.

'No, you don't understand,' he said, his voice beginning to stammer. 'It was just a game we were playing. Pretending we could be together.'

'I think what I overheard happening between the two of you, and what you were both plotting to do, has gone much further then an innocent game.'

His eyes filled with tears and he started to cry, and he looked so young and defenceless she almost reached out to comfort him.

'You do know that Tobiah will discover on his wedding night that Miriam is not a virgin?'

His body convulsed in terror. 'Miriam said it will be all right. That she knows how to make sure Tobiah will never suspect.'

'Do you think she will get away with what she plans to do'

'Yes! I mean, I don't know,' he stammered. 'She believes it will work.'

'Do you love her?'

His voice fell to a whisper. 'I'm not sure. She is strong and wilful and she frightens me sometimes because she gets carried away with her ideas, but I think about her all the time and I love being with her.'

'It is a sinful thing that you are both doing.'

He tried to speak and twice his voice failed him before he got the words out.

'I know.'

She gave a small almost inaudible sigh. 'Listen to me Caleb. It would be better for Tobiah if you and Miriam were to leave the village today before any further harm is done.'

Shocked he stared at her. 'We can't. We have no money. We wouldn't survive.'

'You won't survive here either, once your true connection to Miriam has been uncovered. And it will be when she and Tobiah marry, if not before,' she said dryly. 'Wait here.'

She stood and went quickly into the house, to emerge a few moments later. As she walked back across the courtyard towards him she couldn't help wondering what would become of him, because he was weak and easily led. Miriam, she was certain, would always find a way to survive and get what she wanted.

'Here,' she said holding out the purse of money Varinius had given her. 'Take this. There is enough in the purse for you to leave Sychar with Miriam and make a new life together'

Hardly able to believe his good fortune he stared spellbound at her as he reached out a trembling hand to take the money.

'Have you arranged to see her today?' she asked.

'Yes, I'm taking the goats to graze on the other side of the valley this afternoon. She will meet me there.'

Leah pursed her lips. 'Go now and find her, then leave Sychar quickly. Malachi and Tobiah will be out in the fields until sundown. You will have a good start. Don't delay, because once her father realises that you have both gone he and his sons will come after you.'

The glimmer of hope in his eyes began to dim as she gave her warning. As she walked away she looked back over her shoulder.

'Clear up the broken pieces of pot and bring another jug of milk. And make sure the goats are safely in their pen before you leave.'

He nodded, unable to speak, and he didn't move until he had seen her disappear into the house.

For the next hour she sat at the table, wrestling with her thoughts. In the hope of distracting herself she went out into the courtyard for the milk that Caleb had left under the shade of the palm tree, and carried it into the house. For a while afterwards she stood in the middle of the room motionless, her eyes unseeing, her thoughts turned inwards. Then, with a heavy sigh, she set off for the village and the home of her mother.

Chapter Seventeen

Outside her house Ahava was sitting motionless on a mat in front of her millstone with her chin resting on her chest and her hands clasped loosely in her lap. She felt exhausted and the deadening, lonely weight of isolation oppressed her spirit. She had not seen anyone all morning. Miriam had not arrived to help her with the milling and she reasoned she must have gone with her mother to work in fields. Angrily she dashed away tears of frustration that she could not walk for more than the shortest distance, nor sustain the smallest task without help. With her hands clenched she rubbed her knuckles across her eyes in an effort to clear them, and blinked furiously. She was well aware that she should go indoors, out of the heat, but she felt too exhausted to raise herself.

Somewhere in the village children were playing chase. She could hear their laughter and their voices, high with excitement as they called out to each other.

Seamlessly she drifted into sleep and in her dream she too was running and laughing, a girl again, her body light and swift as she twisted and turned and jumped high into the air. Then the scene dissolved and she was a young bride, standing beside Joseph, with a life full of promise beckoning to her.

In a swirl of mist the image of Joseph began to recede and she cried out as she tried to clutch onto him, but he slipped from her grasp and disappeared. Then the figure of a woman emerged, calling out in a voice that was too faint for her to hear. As the mist cleared she recognised her daughter Judith. With tears streaming down her cheeks and her arms outstretched she struggled to run towards her, but her legs were leaden and no matter how hard she tried she was unable to get any closer.

She awoke with a start, her breathing loud and rapid, and she could feel the palpitations of her heart and the dampness of the perspiration that had broken out on her forehead and across her top lip. As her breathing eased and her heartbeat slowed she became overwhelmed by a deep certainty that something was wrong, very wrong. Malachi had hardly been able to meet her eyes when he and Esther came to tell her that Tobiah and Miriam were betrothed. And Esther had fidgeted uncomfortably. Yet they both knew how much the news would delight her. She felt sure that something was being deliberately hidden from her, something that concerned Tobiah and his happiness.

Feverishly her mind twisted and turned as she sought the answer. She had neither eaten nor drunk since early morning and she reached for her stick, intending to go indoors. Twice she struggled to rise only to fall back again exhausted onto the mat and remain there motionless. Her head began to throb and her vision blurred. When the figure of a woman appeared in front of her, looking down at her with eyes that she recognised, she thought she was seeing an apparition and her heart began to thump again.

'Who are you,' she said, her voice an almost inaudible whisper.

The woman bent towards her and despite how much she struggled to push her away, she found herself lifted by a strong pair of arms and helped into the house, where she was lowered down onto a seat.

She watched, nervously, as the woman filled a cup to the brim with water. Feebly she tried to resist as she put an arm around her shoulders and held it to her lips. Overcome with thirst she drank greedily until it was taken from her. All resistance gone she allowed a cushion to be placed behind her and she lent back into it. As the sweet relief of a cold, wet cloth was put on her head she squeezed her eyes tight shut. When she could bear the suspense no longer she removed the cloth and blinked up at the unsmiling woman in front of her, who steadily returned her look.

'Am I dead?' she asked her.

'No, you are not dead,' the woman replied. 'But it was foolish to sit out in the heat of the mid-day.'

'I don't understand what is happening or how you have come to be here. But it is you, isn't it Leah?' In her confusion and distress she began to tremble and cry.

Leah's smile was forced. 'You do recognise me then?'

'How could I not recognise my own child?' Ahava whispered as she lifted her hands in supplication.

Beyond words the two women stared at each other. Ahava struggled to raise herself and reach out to Leah, who recoiled as though she had been stung. With a long drawn out sigh Ahava sank down again into her seat.

'When did you come back to Sychar?'

'I came home four days ago.' Leah answered sharply.

'But you didn't, did you? You didn't come home so you must be staying somewhere else in the village.' She sat up straight, certain now she knew why Esther and Malachi had been so nervous.

'Do Malachi and Esther know that you are here?'

'Yes they know.'

'Malachi told me you had died in a fire in Caesarea.'

'Well I didn't. But I truly believed that you would be dead by now or I would never have attempted to return,' Leah said, before she could stop herself. She hadn't known that she could be so cruel and she was shocked by the words that had come from her mouth.

Ahava flinched as though she had been struck. Her grief for the loss of this daughter, that she had kept buried in her heart, broke into a flood of pain so acute she rocked forward and wrapped her arms across her chest. As she watched her Leah was filled with a compassion for her mother that surprised her. She knelt and took her in her arms and the thin, fragile feel of Ahava's body, rigid now with fear, caused her to bow her head in shame.

'Where are you staying? Is it with Esther and Malachi?' Ahava whispered, screwing her eyes shut and pulling away a little.

'No. I have been staying in another home.'

'Ahava's eyes snapped open. 'Whose home?' she demanded.

Slowly Leah withdrew her arms and stood up.

'It doesn't matter. All you need to know is that I will be gone soon.'

'Whose home,' Ahava demanded again, her voice stronger now.

'Tobiah's.'

Ahava clutched at her chest.

'Calm yourself. He knows I am your daughter, but not that I am his mother, and it will remain that way.'

'I don't understand, I don't understand,' Ahava repeated, her breath catching on a sob. 'How is it possible for you to be staying with Tobiah.'

Before Leah could answer Esther burst through the doorway. Her veil hung from her shoulders and her hair was in wild disarray. Both her hands were blood stained and there were streaks down the front of her tunic where she had wiped them. All three women remained mute with shock. It was Ahava who recovered first and took charge.

'Sit down Esther. Get her some wine, Leah,' she ordered as she struggled to stand.

With a strength mustered from beyond her physical frame she grasped Esther by her arm, forcing her onto a stool. Taking the wine from Leah she held it to her lips. With feverish mutterings and flailing arms Esther knocked the cup from her hand. As it clattered to the floor she stared down, watching the spilled wine that had puddled in her lap seep through the fabric of her tunic. She felt its wetness on her thighs and she began to laugh hysterically, her eyes roaming wildly around the room. Leah moved quickly and slapped her, leaving the red imprint of her hand on her stricken face. Esther slumped on the stool, her body sagging and her eyes closing.

Ahava's legs began to buckle beneath her and she would have fallen to the floor had Leah not reached out and caught her. Gently she lowered her down onto her chair and placed a shawl around her shoulders before turning back to Esther.

'Open your eyes and look at me' she commanded.

Esther straightened and stared blankly in front of her, the mark of Leah's handprint livid on the pallor of her face. Her mouth moved but no sound came out and she slumped again. Silent tears welled in her eyes and spilled down her cheeks and she buried her head in her hands.

'Look at me Esther,' Leah said, as she bent over her, gently removing her hands from her face. 'Try and tell us what has happened,' she coaxed.

Esther grasped the front of her tunic and pulled her closer, her lips parting and closing again as she struggled to speak. 'I've killed Miriam,' she screamed.

Her voice reverberated around the room and in the shocked silence that followed the only sound was Ahava's laboured breathing. Leah was the first to recover. She filled another cup with wine and offered it again to Esther. Her hand shook as she reached for it and it chinked against her teeth as she took a long drink, dribbles running down her chin.

Leah went to her mother's side and took both her hands in hers. They were cold and clammy and she rubbed them until the colour returned and they began to warm. Ahava gripped her wrist and pulled her down onto the stool beside her and they both stared at Esther. In a low, flat voice she began to tell them what she had done.

From sunrise she had been out working in the fields, gleaning. When she began to feel unwell she decided to return home. As she approached her house she was surprised to see the door standing open. She thought that Miriam had returned early from helping Ahava with the milling and she smiled, happy that that her daughter was home. She was about to call out to her, when she heard voices coming from the room at the back of the house. She stood rooted to the spot, listening to the throaty tenor of a man's voice and the ecstatic moans of her daughter. With a cry like a wounded animal she rushed in to find Miriam and Caleb lying naked and writhing in each other's arms. Over Caleb's shoulder Miriam saw her.

In a blind rage she snatched up the water pitcher standing on a chest. Holding it high above her head she ran shrieking at a terrified Caleb. Before she could strike Miriam had covered him with her body, her arms outstretched, screaming for her mother to stop as the blow came crashing down. With blood spurting from her nose she fell backwards her eyes closing. Caleb struggled out from beneath her.

Dropping to her knees beside Miriam she scooped her up into her arms, sobbing that it wasn't her she had intended to hurt. Frantically she had tried to stem the flow of blood with her hands whilst Caleb cowered in a corner, shocked and speechless. Certain that Miriam was dead she struggled to her feet and raced towards Ahava's house.

With mounting horror Leah and Ahava had listened to her story and now the silence in the room was suffocating. Freeing herself from her mother's hand, still clenched around her wrist, Leah went to stand in front of Esther who stared up at her vacantly. Taking her by her shoulders she squeezed gently.

'Stay here both of you,' she ordered, before running from the house. The two women sat in silence for what seemed like an eternity until Leah returned. As she came through the door Esther stood up, her eyes fixed in a wide, beseeching stare.

'She isn't dead,' Leah said, flatly.

Esther rocked back on her heels with a low, soft wail.

'I must go to her. I must go to my daughter.'

Leah held out an arm to stop her. 'It's no use Esther, Miriam isn't there. Both she and Caleb have gone. They have taken Malachi's mule and left. She couldn't have been hurt as badly as you thought.'

Chapter Eighteen

Leah made Ahava as comfortable as she could by placing a low stool beneath her feet and a cushion behind her back. After promising to return quickly she put an arm around Esther's waist and guided her from the house. Once outside they stood blinking in the sun, neither feeling any warmth from the scorching heat of its rays.

Slowly they made their way through the dusty, empty streets. The rising wail of a crying baby mingling with the distant rhythmic bleating of sheep, grazing on the hillside, added to the strange unreality of the moment. As they approached the house Esther stopped and clutched at Leah's arm and her hand felt cold and clammy.

'I don't want to go in,' she said.

Without answering Leah thrust her forward through the open doorway. Once inside Esther clung to her. Slowly and firmly Leah prised herself free and went to fill a bowl with water, placing it on the table. Esther stood still and compliant whilst she removed her tunic and washed away the dried blood and wine stains from her hands and legs. When it was done she slipped a clean tunic over head.

'You need to lie down and rest for a while,' Leah urged, putting a firm arm around her waist as she led her towards the bedroom. 'Tell me what herbs to use and I'll make up a potion to help you sleep.'

Esther pulled away. The colour had returned to her cheeks and there was a spark of anger in her eyes.

'I don't think that I will ever sleep or feel warm again. My daughter is betrothed to Tobiah and she has lain with another man. When her father discovers the shame she has brought upon his family his anger will be great. He will call on our sons to help him find her and if they do…'

She began to sob so pitifully that Leah took her in her arms, holding her close, until out of exhaustion she quietened. Gently she eased her down onto the mattress and knelt beside her. For a long while Esther lay still and unmoving, staring up at the ceiling, her hand limp in Leah's. The weight of the silence bore down oppressively around them. Slowly Esther's eyes became heavy and closed and Leah freed her hand. After a moments hesitation she got up off her knees and made her way towards the door. She was almost there when she was drawn to a halt by the sound of Esther's voice, grating and anguished, as she struggled to sit up.

'How could Miriam behave in such a way Leah? How could she be so wicked? My daughter has sinned and shamed herself and her family by what she has done. It is right that Malachi and our sons should try to find her and that she should be punished for her sin.'

Leah went back and knelt once more at her side, taking her hand again.

'I don't believe that it is right, Esther. I have no affection for your daughter because there is a wildness in her that may one day destroy her, and perhaps those close to her too. But I wouldn't want to see her murdered in such a brutal way.'

Esther's face registered her shock. 'You know that it wouldn't be murder. She is betrothed to Tobiah and she has committed adultery. In the Law, Moses has ordered us to stone to death women who behave in the way she has.'

Leah was about to reply when Esther put up a trembling hand to stop her.

'I would have thought that you, of all people, would want to see Tobiah avenged after what Miriam and Caleb have done. They have betrayed and hurt him, just when he thought he might be finding happiness again.'

'I think Miriam would have hurt Tobiah much more if she had married him,' Leah said quietly.

Taking deep, shuddering breaths Esther began tugging at her hair, pulling out thick strands.

'If she is found I shall have to bear witness to what she has done before the elders of the village. They will condemn her because of my testimony.'

She began to wail as she rocked violently back and forth. Leah caught both her wrists and held her tight and Esther's eyes pleaded for reassurance as they met hers. 'She and Caleb might escape. They might not be found,' she said pitifully.

Leah loosened her grip. 'Yes, Esther they might.'

For a fleeting moment she felt a hot flush of guilt about the money she had given Caleb, quickly followed by relief that she had. Now Esther and Malachi would never discover just how much their scheming daughter was truly capable of and Tobiah would not be destroyed by marrying her.

Esther buried her head in her hands. 'Miriam is strong willed. I have always known that. But I cannot believe she has behaved like a harlot.' She looked up at Leah and her voice hardened. 'She told me how happy she was to become betrothed to Tobiah and then she committed adultery in her father's house. Whether you think it right, or not, if she is found she must punished.'

'What about the grace of forgiveness Esther? Isn't that also written in the Books of the Law? Perhaps it isn't God demanding such cruel retribution but the men who use Him to fulfil their own desires for domination and vengeance.' Leah said dryly.

Esther stared at her as she considered what she had just heard. Slowly her face crumpled and flushed with fear.

'I don't understand what you mean.'

Leah sighed. 'I think perhaps you don't want to.'

Esther's breathing became uneven and heavy as she scrubbed the tears from her cheeks with the palms of her hands, and her face took on a hard, determined look.

'I don't want you talking to me like that. I won't listen. Malachi would forbid me to see you again if he knew, and you would not be welcome in our home.'

Before Leah could reply Esther grabbed the front of her tunic and pulled her closer.

'You are a hypocrite,' she spat, masking her own pain by attacking Leah. 'You talk about forgiveness and yet you have no compassion in your heart for your mother.'

Leah's face became pinched as she recognised the truth in what Esther had said. For a moment she felt overwhelmed by the complexity of her feelings.

Esther gripped her tighter. 'Surely you know she and Joseph thought they were doing their best for you when they arranged your marriage. It wasn't their fault that your husband turned out to be so cruel.'

'You know nothing about it,' Leah said softly as she prised Esther's hands off her.

'I know that I don't understand you. Right up until the time you left for Caesarea, we all begged you to see your parents and you turned your face away. You didn't even shed a tear when we told you your brother Reuben had died of plague.'

'I already knew Reuben was dead. When the plague left the land, and people began travelling again, my mother got a message to me.' Her voice began to shake. 'She asked me to send a message back letting her know that I was well.'

'And did you?'

Leah held her gaze and swallowed hard. 'No, I did not.' She had to look away then because of the turmoil inside her and the contempt on Esther's face.

'You were always a strange child, Leah, but I have never thought you cruel. I do now.'

'You didn't think I was cruel then, when I left my son, not three years old, with my sister and her husband?'

Esther's expression softened. 'No Leah. I didn't understand it but I knew you were trying to do your best for Tobiah. I saw the look of pain on your face when Judith came to the door holding him in her arms, as you were about to leave. I prayed then that you would be safe and find happiness in your new life.'

Nervously she began twisting her hands. 'Why were you with your mother just now, if not to make your peace with her?'

'Because there are questions I need answers to.' Leah snapped, before she could stop herself.

'Oh Leah!' Esther gave a long, shuddering sigh as she pushed back her hair that was lying lank across her shoulders. Her face was drawn and grey and there were black smudges beneath her eyes. Utterly worn out she slumped down onto the mattress and turned on her side, her back to Leah.

'Poor Tobiah; so gentle and so kind,' she whispered. 'He doesn't deserve what Miriam has done. I can't bear to think what it will do to him.'

'His pride will be wounded but he will recover,' Leah said sharply.

Covering her face with her hands Esther began to cry and Leah watched her helplessly.

'You and I should not be quarrelling, Esther. Try to sleep a little. I need to go back to Ahava now. She has suffered two shocks today and shouldn't be left alone for much longer. When I've settled her I will go to the fields and tell Malachi he needs to come home.'

She felt Esther's shudder of fear as she covered her with a blanket and pulled it up around her shoulders. Although there was no one else to overhear, she bent down until her lips were close to her ear.

'I will delay as long as I can so that Miriam and Caleb get a good start,' she said softly.

Esther's tears turned into wailing sobs that she tried to muffle in the blanket.

Chapter Nineteen

Leah drew her veil across her face and lowered her head as she came out of Esther's house into the shimmering brightness of the sun. She was acutely conscious of the old women, sitting in their doorways, who had been left looking after the small children whilst their mother's worked in fields. Their eyes were avid with curiosity as they followed her. They had been witness to what had happened at Malachi's house and she could feel their shocked excitement at the enormity of it all, and their puzzlement about her. She knew that when their daughters and granddaughters returned home the gossip would rebound around the courtyards and provide endless speculation at the well the next morning.

Walking without haste and looking neither left nor right she reached her mother's home and slipped inside. Ahava was still sitting where she had left her, with her eyes closed. Her breathing was shallow and her veil had slipped revealing her hair, white and sparse, and lying flattened to her scalp. The skin on her face was almost transparent in its thinness and a thin trickle of saliva was dribbling from the corner of her mouth, on to her chin.

Leah moved to her side and placed her hand gently on her shoulder, shocked once more by the feel of the slender, bird like frame beneath her fingers. As she looked down on her she felt a welling up of such pain and sadness she thought her heart might stop.

Sensing her presence Ahava stirred and for a moment she appeared not to know were she was. As her eyes began to focus and rest on her daughter she lifted up thin, shaking arms towards her.

'Come and sit by me, Leah. There is much that you and I need to talk about.'

Leah fought down the desire to throw herself into her mother's arms and weep until she had no more tears left. Instead she drew back.

'I have to find Malachi and tell him he needs to go home to Esther,' she said wearily.

'How is Esther?'

'She's sleeping, but she shouldn't be left alone for too long.'

Ahava rubbed at her eyes with her knuckles until they were red and watery. Her veil had slipped and she pulled it up over her head.

'Don't worry. If she wakes before Malachi arrives home she will make her way back here. She will need to be with a friend.'

She looked towards Leah and then at the footstool by her feet. Leah sat down without a murmur, wondering how it was that after all these years, and all that she had known and done, she should feel like a child again in the presence of this small, frail woman.

'I am tired, Leah, and my time is short. I thought never to see you again, but God has blessed me. Now we need to try and put right all that has been wrong between us, before it is too late. Tell me what happened to you, after you left Tobiah with Judith and Thomas, and how, after all these years, you came to be back in Sychar and living in his home.'

Leah allowed the silence to fill the room before she spoke.

'I will tell you. But first I need to know why, after my brother Reuben raped me and I conceived Tobiah by him, my father sold me into slavery. Because that is what I can't forgive you for.' Her voice broke. 'I was barely thirteen.'

She shifted her gaze as Ahava took her chin in her hand, holding her firmly.

'Look at me,' she said sharply. 'Joseph did not sell you.'

Slowly and deliberately Leah removed her mother's hand from her face and laid it back in her lap, glancing sideways at her. Ahava gave a soft gasp.

'What beautiful eyes you have. Just like his,'

Leah frowned, and feeling of unease stirred in her.

'Just like whose?' she snapped.

To late to draw back Ahava took a deep breath and said the words she had never thought to utter.

'Your father's.'

'My father had small eyes. They were dark, almost black. I look nothing like him at all.'

'Joseph was not your father.'

Leah stared at her mother in disbelief as she struggled to make sense of what she had heard.

'Who are you, old woman. I don't know you. No wonder I always felt he hated me.' She fought against the urge to grab her mother by her shoulders and shake her. 'He did know, didn't he, that I was not his child?'

Ahava lowered her head, unable to meet her eyes.

'Answer me.'

'Yes, he knew. And he did not hate you Leah. Joseph was incapable of hating. But he found it hard to love you because every time he looked at you he saw your father, and it reminded him of what I had done. And I have paid for it, every moment of my life since.'

Leah pressed her fingers to her temples as her head began to ache. 'You have paid,' she said with such bitterness that Ahava winced. 'The man I believed to be my father could not bear me near him and you pushed me away from your knee whenever he was around. I think I paid the price for your sin too mother.'

The room seemed to get hotter and the throbbing in her head became stronger.

'I suppose that was why Reuben thought it safe to torment me throughout my childhood. Because he knew I was unloved.'

'That isn't true. I loved you from the moment you were born,' Ahava said, in a ragged whisper.

'Well I never felt your love. The only joy in my life, as a child, was the affection of my sister who tried to protect me from Reuben's sly punches and kicks. When she married he was free to torment me as he wished. The only time my father... The only time Joseph ever defended me was when he heard my screams coming from the barn as Reuben raped me, and he ran in to drag him off. When he beat him with the whip he kept by the door I rejoiced in every blow, until you came to prevent him from being killed.'

Each word fell on Ahava's ears like a hammer blow, and she put both hands across her mouth to stifle the sobs that were threatening to engulf her.

'I needed you to hold me in your arms and tell me everything would be all right; that you would keep me safe,' Leah said, her voice breaking. 'But you didn't. I believed then that you thought I was to blame. I was terrified of what might happen to me. I thought I might be driven from the village or worse. And no one comforted me.'

'I couldn't hold you Leah, because you shrank from my touch like a wounded animal and turned your face from me. Your eyes were so wide with fear, and you looked so fragile, I thought if I were to take you in my arms you would shatter into a thousand fragments. Both Joseph and I knew you were not to blame. What Reuben did to you almost killed me, and it broke Joseph's heart. He cursed his son and never spoke to him again. And neither did I. Not even when he lay dying of plague, begging for my forgiveness and for that of his father, and screaming out for yours.'

Leah gave a mirthless laugh that ended on a dry sob. Then she had to bury her head in her hands to escape the naked agony on her mother's face.

'If Reuben crying out for my forgiveness is supposed to console me, then I can tell you it does not,' she said, as she lifted her head.

'You watched me like a hawk afterwards. As soon as you suspected I was with child Joseph made arrangements to sell me to his cousin Sarah and her husband, so that I could look after them in their old age. When he took me on that long journey to their village he spoke not one word of consolation to me as he left me with them.'

She felt neither pain nor anger just a desolate emptiness.

'He couldn't Leah. He couldn't look at you without being reminded of what his son had done and the shame he felt. But he did not sell you to them. If they told you that they lied. He gave them money, almost everything he had, so they would care for you and the baby when it was born. And he told them he was entrusting you to them. We thought we were acting for the best, that you would be safe and might become a daughter to them. Sarah and Ephraim had always longed for a child but Sarah was barren.'

As her words tumbled over each other Leah's eyes narrowed to slits.

'Why did you lie and tell them I had been raped by a stranger whilst I was out alone in the fields. Was it to protect Reuben?'

'No, it was not to protect Reuben. It was to protect you and the baby when it was born. The stigma of being a child conceived by rape would be bad enough, but the stigma of being the child of your mother's brother would bring even greater shame and abhorrence.

We were grateful to Sarah and Ephraim for being prepared to accept you into their home and agreeing to look after you and the baby.'

'And Joseph told everyone in the village he had arranged my betrothal and I had gone to live with my future husband's family until we married.'

'We thought we were doing the best for you, Leah. When plague swept the land a few months later there was so much grief in the countryside for those who had died, no one thought to ask about you. Afterwards, when it was over, Joseph told Judith he had received a message saying you had married. When you came back to Sychar with Tobiah, everyone believed he was the son of your husband.'

She paused as she saw a flicker of anger in Leah's eyes and she had to force herself to go on before she lost courage.

'It broke my heart when you left again, refusing to see me. My only consolation was I could nurse my grandson.'

'You and Joseph didn't see Tobiah as an abomination then, because he was the child of my brother?' Leah said, her look withering.

'No Leah, we did not.'

'How well it turned out for you all: Joseph had a grandson to inherit the farm and you and my sister had my child to love. I knew it would be safe to leave Tobiah with her and Thomas because neither you nor Joseph would ever reveal the truth about him to anyone. Your web of lies served you well. And I kept up the pretence.'

Ahava's eyes begged for understanding as she looked at her daughter but Leah could not allow herself to be deflected by pity.

'Shall I tell you what happened to me after Joseph left me with Ephraim and Sarah?' she said, through tight lips. 'They treated me as a slave right up to the time Tobiah was born. Afterwards Sarah sat nursing him all day, whilst I cooked and cleaned the house and worked alongside Ephraim and his brother Eli on their patch of land. When Tobiah was three months old Sarah died and a short time afterwards Ephraim forced me to marry him. He thought I would give him the child Sarah had never been able to conceive. Each time I failed he beat me. When he became sick, he cursed me on his deathbed.' She paused and screwed her eyes tight shut.

Ahava crossed her arms over her breast, as though shielding herself from a blow, 'Go on, Leah,' she whispered.

'After Ephraim was buried Eli took me in marriage, because Levirate law says if a man dies childless his brother should marry his widow, and their first son should be called after the dead brother, to carry on his name.

'He was old and ugly and smelled from the putrid, running sores on his legs. He allowed me just enough food to live on and he begrudged Tobiah every mouthful. I didn't conceive with him either. On the day I found him beating my son I made up my mind to run away.

'That night, whilst Eli was asleep and snoring, I strapped Tobiah onto the back of his mule and left. Somehow I managed to get us both to Sychar. Judith was distraught when she saw how bruised, starving and thin we were.'

Ahava's face had become ashen as she listened. Panic-stricken Leah shook her arm.

'Do not die now. You still have much to tell me. Who was my father?'

'He was a merchant from across the Jordan. When he came to the farm with his small caravan of camels and asked if he could water the animals and take lodgings in our barn for the night, Joseph was happy to oblige because he paid well.'

She began to pluck at the skin on her throat and Leah watched, hypnotised by the rhythmic movement of her hand.

'For years my life had been unbearable. Joseph had become impotent shortly after Reuben was born and had withdrawn into himself. He would go months without speaking to me or looking at me. And when he did it was to rebuke or beat me for some imagined fault he had found me guilty of. But for most of the time he acted as though I didn't exist.'

'So you decided to turn to another man. What was the name of this merchant who was my father?'

Ahava plucked again at the skin on her throat as she struggled to say the name she driven from her memory for so many years.

'His name was Ishmael. After the first time he took lodgings with us, he began to come regularly to the farm. He was always courteous and grateful for the meals I provided and I basked in the small attentions he gave me. I felt alive again after the painful years of loneliness. As time went by the feelings he aroused in me grew stronger. But as long he didn't guess I thought there would be no harm done.

'When he was due to arrive Joseph would kill a lamb that he had been fattening and roast it and I would prepare a meal. Then they would sit together, laughing, talking and drinking our best wine. As I watched Joseph it seemed as though the man I had married and loved had come back to me. Yet never once did he return my look or give me a kind word. But the eyes of the man who was enjoying his hospitality constantly sought mine. Eyes just like yours Leah. They followed me, caressed me and drew me to him. I would feel myself trembling with desire for him. And he knew.

'Each time he left to travel home I would be in turmoil. I began to obsess about him and fear him too. Yet I longed for the time when he would visit again. And when that time came I was filled with an excitement and a dread that left me feeling weak and sick and Joseph never seemed to notice or to care.'

'So you committed adultery and I was the result.'

'It sounds so hard and cold when you say it like that Leah. My husband, the man I had once been so cherished and loved by, appeared to hate me and I couldn't understand why.

'All through the first ten years of our marriage, when I didn't conceive, he had remained loving and consoling, never once blaming me, or saying an unkind word. And even though his father demanded that he divorce me and marry another woman, or take a concubine to give him children, he defied him. When finally I bore Joseph a daughter and then a son, he was overjoyed. We were happier than we had ever been until he became impotent and turned against me, cruelly shutting me out. He wouldn't believe that it didn't matter to me. That I loved him still.'

'Not enough to prevent you from doing what you did,' Leah snapped.

Ahava took a sharp intake of breath. 'You don't need to tell me how sinfully I behaved, Leah. I gave way to a passion born out of loneliness and heartache and I suffered for that sin. You would need to walk in my shoes to understand.'

Leah lowered her head, shamed by the hidden secrets of her own past and her hypocrisy in judging her mother.

'How long did it go on for, you and this merchant?'

'It was just that once. It happened two years after his first visit. We were expecting him and he arrived late in the afternoon. Shortly afterwards Joseph was called away to help with a sheep that was having difficulty lambing. Ishmael offered to go with him but he refused to let him.' Her brow furrowed as though she were trying to work out a puzzle.

'The strange thing is, before Joseph left he looked at me for a moment as though he was really seeing me once more. He smiled and there were tears in his eyes, but then they went hard and cold again. He told Ishmael to make himself comfortable and that I would serve food and drink, and then he left without a backward glance. He was gone for three hours. After that day Ishmael never returned to the farm again, either out of shame for what had happened between us during those hours or because he had achieved what he desired. I like to think it was for the first reason.'

'Did he have a wife and family?'

She waited impatiently for Ahava to answer

'Yes, he had a wife and children.'

'I really don't know who you are. You are my mother and you are a stranger.' Her voice grated.

'Does anyone ever really know another person, Leah? Do we even know ourselves until something happens to put us to the test?'

Struggling between wanting to condemn her mother for what she had done and the bitter knowledge of her own past sins, Leah remained silent.

'There is something that I have never understood,' Ahava said quietly, as though speaking to herself. 'After Ishmael left the farm the following day Joseph came and held me in his arms for a long time, and I thought my heart would break. When I began to cry and try to confess to what I had done, he refused to allow me to speak. He kept telling me to hush and he placed his hand, very gently, across my mouth to silence me. By then he was crying too. Afterwards it was as though the misery of the past five years had never happened because the loving, gentle man I had married had returned to me. But my sin weighed heavily. And then I found I was to have a child.

'For days I brooded, terrified for what I knew would be my fate, and distraught that my children would be left without a mother when

I was stoned to death for my adultery. Somehow I found the courage to tell Joseph and I expected him to raise his hand to me, but he didn't. He stayed silent for a long time. When he finally spoke, I had to strain to hear him, because his voice was so low.'

She drifted into silence and Leah leaned forward to shake her arm.

'What did he say?'

'He said that he loved me.'

Her face had filled with a look of such wonder and softness that Leah caught her breath.

'He put his hand on my stomach and whispered that perhaps when the child was born it would be a girl and she would look like me. I tried to thank him but he refused to let me say another word. He never once mentioned your father again, although he always lay between us like a ghost.'

'But I didn't look like you, did I? I looked like Ishmael. No wonder Joseph hated me.'

'He didn't hate you, Leah. I have already told you he wasn't capable of hating. But each time he saw me nursing you, or playing with you, I could tell by the look in his eyes that he thought I was seeing and wanting Ishmael. I wasn't able to reassure him because by then he had built a wall around what had happened that was too high to climb. The burden of shame was mine, and it was a heavy load to carry. Yet when Joseph lay dying he begged for my forgiveness. And even to this day I don't know what it was that he was asking my forgiveness for.'

'Perhaps it was for the way he treated you when he became impotent, and for deliberately encouraging Ishmael to come to your home after he had guessed what he was doing. He knew he should have protected you, not left you alone with him. He might also have been sorry for punishing you, by making you afraid to love me.'

Beyond tears Ahava sat with her head bowed and Leah knelt at her knee and took her in her arms, holding her tight against her breast. Gently she stroked back the fine wisps of hair standing up on her head, and then let her rest back in her chair whilst she went to fill a cup with water. She smiled as she gave it to her and Ahava's eyes, wide and luminous, sought hers as she drank.

'I must go to the fields now and find Malachi and Tobiah and tell them what has happened,' she said, taking the empty cup from her mother's hands. 'Afterwards I shall come back and stay the night. I won't leave you alone,'

Spent of emotion Ahava leant back in her chair.

'I'm so grateful that my prayers have been answered and that God has sent you back to me before I die. I have always loved, you Leah,' she whispered, as her eyes began to close.

Chapter Twenty

The heat of the day was cooling and sunset was only an hour away, as Leah made her way towards Tobiah's grain fields. The thought of telling both him and Malachi that Miriam and Caleb had run away together weighed heavily on her and her feet dragged. Yet she could not regret her part in it because it meant that Tobiah was safe from Miriam and Miriam was safe from the fate of being stoned to death that inevitably would have awaited her.

It would have been so much worse for everyone, she reasoned, if Tobiah had married the girl and she had carried out her plan. But she could find no comfort in this thought and she wrapped her arms across her body as she walked in an effort to dispel the feeling of despair that was threatening to engulf her.

Carried on the breeze she heard the voices of the reapers calling to each other as they moved through the waving barley, grabbing the last clumps of heavy headed stalks and cutting them free with their sickles. As she drew closer she could see the gleaners behind them, bent double, gathering up what had fallen from the sheaves. At the corners of the field the widows and the women from the poorer families of the village had gathered in groups, waiting patiently for the time they could help themselves to any grain left lying on the ground. She felt their hostile stares and heard their deliberately loud speculation about her, as she went to stand beneath the shade of a palm tree.

On the far side of the field Tobiah and Malachi stood together, watching as the last loads were put into the cart of a patiently waiting mule. When it was done Tobiah signalled a young boy to take it to the threshing floor on the western side of the village, where the winds, blowing in from the Great Sea, would aid the winnowing of the grain.

With immeasurable sadness she saw the two men clasp each other around the shoulders, in an act of friendship and closeness she knew might be destroyed forever by what had happened.

Malachi's face was covered with a beam of satisfaction as he looked out across the harvested field. He flexed his aching muscles and called to the waiting women to begin picking up the leftovers lying on the ground and then he caught sight of her. He raised a hand to shade his eyes and the smile left his face as he leaned in towards Tobiah to whisper in his ear.

She felt a deep ache as she watched them walking determinedly towards her, their faces set in angry lines. The noisy, good-natured shouting and laughter of the labourers, who were standing around in groups, began to slowly die and then rise again as they made forced attempts at pretending nothing unusual was happening.

The women who had been gleaning and who were now ladling fresh water into cups from large earthenware pitchers, stopped what they were doing, their eyes gleaming bright with curiosity, as they watched Tobiah and Malachi cross the field. Leah's sense of wretchedness increased as she saw the anxiety in both their faces. When Malachi stopped directly in front of her and grabbed her shoulder she thought he was about to hit her, instead he dropped his arm and glared at her in disbelief.

'Why have you come here?' he hissed. 'Don't you care that talk of you will be all over the village by tonight, and that it will reach Ahava by the morning? Then she will start asking questions.'

Leah lifted her chin and the mesmerising force of her eyes unnerved him. 'There is no need for concern about Ahava. I've been with her for most of the day,' she said.

Both men stared at her in surprise. Then as Tobiah grasped the implications of what she had said, he gave her a smile that lit up the soberness of his face and he nodded his approval.

'Why? Why would you do that?' Malachi asked unaware of the unspoken exchange that had passed between her and Tobiah. 'You have been so adamant in your refusal to see her.'

Before she could answer Tobiah was jolted by a sense of shock as he realised that if she had left Ahava to come to the fields, something must be very wrong.

'Is my grandmother all right,' he demanded, his voice sharp with anxiety.

'Yes, she is well.' She turned towards Malachi. 'But you must to go home now, Esther needs you.'

He shook his head in bewilderment. 'I knew she felt unwell and had stopped gleaning earlier, but I didn't think it was anything to worry about. Is our daughter looking after her?'

'No, Miriam isn't with her mother.'

She avoided meeting his eyes and he was filled with a deep sense of foreboding.

'Where is she then? Has something happened to her?'

'I'm sorry, Malachi. You need to hear it from Esther not from me.' He grasped her arm and she felt the tremble in him.

'Go home, Malachi,' Tobiah said softly. 'And you Leah, go to my house. I will join you later after I have paid the labourers their wages.'

As Tobiah walked swiftly back across the field Malachi released his grip on her arm, his expression a mixture of pleading and fear.

'What has Miriam done, Leah?'

She couldn't answer and he ran his tongue around his dry lips. Drawing on every shred of dignity he could muster he straightened his shoulders, and without another word set off towards the village with deliberately unhurried strides.

As she watched him go, her part in what had happened bore down on her once more. Then she recalled the image of the broken, bleeding body of a young woman, lying in a shallow pit, stoned to death after being accused and convicted of adultery. Her head was smashed to a pulp and the socket of one eye lay empty, her other eye rested grotesquely where her cheek should have been. One arm lay palm up in a protective gesture across her breast. The other, dislocated by a blow to her shoulder was thrown outwards at an awkward angle. Three fingers on her hand were curled in towards her palm, and the fourth appeared to be pointing accusingly towards the men surrounding her, still holding rocks in their hands. She shuddered at the memory. Whatever Miriam had done she believed she was right in trying to save her from that, and to save Tobiah from her.

The light was beginning to fade as she reached the house and inside it felt stifling. She stood in the middle of the floor, unmoving, until her eyes grew accustomed to the dimness of the room. After a while she lit a small oil lamp and carried it out into the courtyard, placing it carefully on a low stool beside the wooden bench. She sat and folded her hands in her lap, allowing her mind to drift, not wanting to dwell on the pain she was going to inflict when she told Tobiah that Miriam and Caleb had run away together.

As she waited she became aware that too much time had elapsed. The labourers would have all gone home for their suppers by now and yet still Tobiah had not returned. She shifted, uneasily, wondering if she should go back to the fields to look for him. Then she saw him standing at the entrance to the courtyard, his face hidden in shadow. A breeze stirred the leaves of the myrtle bush and the scent from the flowers drifted towards her as the lamp flickered and went out.

He avoided looking at her as he walked past her into the house with the dog bounding ahead of him. For a while she could hear him talking to the animal as he moved around, and then there was silence. When he finally emerged a pale, silver moon had risen and the first stars were beginning to shine. He crossed the space between them and sat beside her. As his eyes sought hers she could see only their darkness.

'I am glad you reconsidered and went to see my grandmother,' he said. 'I hope you and she have been able to put right what was wrong between you. Now, tell me, Leah, what is it that Miriam has done? Run off with Caleb?'

She shivered, although she wasn't cold, and she wondered, not for the first time, at the sensitive perceptions of this gentle man who was her son.

'How did you know?'

His laugh was bitter. 'When you told Malachi she wasn't with her mother, I could tell by the expression on your face that something serious had happened. So serious you couldn't bear to say what it was nor could you look Malachi in the eye. I knew then that Caleb was involved.'

Unconsciously she lifted her hand to stroke his face and then she drew back, his natural dignity stilling her action before it had properly begun.

'I couldn't tell you both in the field with all the labourers watching. Malachi needed to hear it from Esther. She is distraught with the shock of what their daughter has done and with fear for what will happen if he finds her and Caleb.'

'I am certain he and his sons will try. And you know what will happen if they do.'

He laughed again and the sound jarred on her. Then his body began to shake and she felt an overwhelming ache to hold and comfort him.

'She spoke about Caleb when we returned from burying your son. I saw the smile on her lips and the expression on her face as she said his name, and her fear when she admitted he had been in the house alone with her. I sensed then there was something between them, but I chose to ignore it. In fact, I persuaded Malachi her indiscretion had been an innocent attempt to befriend him. I had made up my mind to marry her and I didn't want anything to get in the way of it. I should have trusted my feelings.'

He sat clenching and unclenching his fists. Leah took his hands in hers, holding them tight until he pulled free.

'They won't survive. Caleb has neither trade nor any means of supporting her. I dread to think what this will do to Malachi and Esther.'

Once again she felt a rising guilt about the money she had given to Caleb.

In the doorway of the house, two yellow eyes glittered in the moonlight, attracting her attention. The dark shape of the dog crossed the courtyard to sink down beside Tobiah, pawing gently at his leg. He ran his hand in long rhythmic strokes across its back and she saw the tension in his body begin to ease.

'I am glad you decided to make your peace with my grandmother. How is she?' The rough edge had lifted from his voice.

'She is angered by what Miriam has done and worried about you.'

He shifted on the seat and she tried to catch his expression as he turned his head away.

'Tell her I too am angry and my pride is hurt. But I will recover.' He got up from the bench and immediately the dog sprang to his side. 'She shouldn't be left alone for much longer. She will be anxious and need to be reassured.'

'I have promised to spend the night with her,' Leah said, as she rose to her feet.

Helplessly they stood facing each other until Tobiah took charge.

'Let me re-light the lamp, whilst you put a change of clothes in a bag. Then I'll walk with you to the bottom of the olive grove. Tell my grandmother that I will see her tomorrow.'

Chapter Twenty-One

Leah arrived at her mother's home to find the lamps lit and the table laid with a bowl of roasted grains, a platter of cheese and a basket of flat bread, with olive oil for dipping. There was also a cake of dried fruit and two cups filled to the brim with wine. Ahava was sitting in her chair dozing, her hands folded in her lap.

Careful not to make a noise that might startle her mother she crossed the floor and stood looking down at her. Ahava muttered in her sleep and shifted her position then her eyes fluttered open. For a moment she appeared not to know who Leah was. Her dawning recognition and smile of joy was quickly replaced by a frown of anxiety. As she struggled to rise to her feet and keep her balance, Leah reached out to steady her.

'How is Tobiah? Have you told him what has happened?' she asked, her voice anxious.

'Yes, I have, and he is concerned more for you, Esther and Malachi than he is for himself.' She bent forward she brushed away a tear from Ahava's cheek. 'He will visit you tomorrow. Let me help you to the table. You haven't eaten since morning and neither have I.'

She filled a bowl with grains laying it in front of her mother, and then another for herself, all the while conscious that Ahava's eyes were following her every movement. Her hand shook as she took a long drink from her cup of wine. As it curled around her stomach, the sick, cold feeling that had been gripping her began to ebb. She picked at the food finding it surprisingly good.

'So like Tobiah, always more concerned for other people than for himself,' Ahava murmured, between mouthfuls.

'Yes, he has grown into a fine man. You and my sister raised him well.'

Leah's voice was edged with a forced brightness and she turned her head, not wanting her mother to see the mixture of pain and bitterness on her face that she was finding difficult to conceal.

'He shouldn't be alone now,' Ahava said anxiously. 'Go back, when you have finished supper, and stay with him. I would go with you if I could walk that far.'

Leah managed to smile as she laid a hand on top of her mother's. 'He's not alone; the dog is there.'

Ahava sighed. 'Yes, of course! That animal is a great comfort to him. What do you think will happen now, Leah?' Does Tobiah intend go with Malachi in search of Miriam and Caleb?'

'No, he said he wouldn't.'

'I can hardly believe the harm that wicked girl has done. She always seemed so sweet and innocent. I never would have thought her capable of such a thing.'

Leah looked at her for a moment, unsmiling. 'People aren't always whom they appear to be. Are they, mother?'

Ahava gasped and her hands fluttered to her lips. Ashamed of the pain she had just inflicted Leah wished she could draw back the words. She gathered her mother in her arms and held her.

'I'm sorry, I didn't mean to hurt you.'

'I know that. But what you say is true. I am certainly not the woman you thought I was.'

Their eyes met and held and Leah looked away first. 'You are worn out and you need to sleep. Let me help you to bed,' she said.

Unresisting Ahava lent on her arm, allowing herself to be led into the bedroom. After settling her on the mattress Leah dowsed one of the lamps, leaving the other one lit. For a moment she hesitated, then she lay down and pulled the blanket up, tucking it around her mother's shoulders. She was almost asleep when she felt Ahava plucking at her hand.

'Leah, I want you to tell me where you have been all these years, and what happened to you,' she said, her voice drowsy.

After a long pause Leah answered. 'I will tell you, tomorrow. But for now we must both rest.'

There was no reply from Ahava, just a soft snuffling snore. Leah smiled and wrapped an arm around her and her throat ached with unshed tears as she remembered her childhood yearnings to be held in the safety of this woman's arms. Now it was she, the daughter, who had become comforter to the mother.

When she awoke she knew the hour was late but she was in no hurry to rise. She lay quite still, allowing herself to drift between sleep and consciousness, aware of the warmth of her mother's body beside her and a sense of comfort and belonging that she didn't want to let go of.

Imperceptibly, thoughts of all that had happened since the morning she and Daniel had escaped from Marcellus began to seep into her mind. As they became an unbearable torrent she rose from the bed and bent over her mother, stroking her face until she opened her eyes. Immediately Ahava gave a wide smile of recognition and Leah bent to kiss her cheek.

'Good, you are awake,' she said. 'It's getting late and Tobiah will be here soon to see you. Before we have breakfast let me help you wash and then I'll bring you a clean tunic to wear.'

'No thank you! I can manage to wash myself, if you bring me a bowl of water.'

Leah laughed, relieved to see that her spirit had returned and Ahava laughed too.

The morning was well advanced when she went outside to light the bread oven. As she looked up she saw Tobiah approaching with long, determined strides. He stopped in front of her and she anxiously searched his face for signs of strain. As his eyes met and held hers she was relieved to see the calmness in him and his unforced smile.

'Your grandmother slept well last night and she is waiting for you,' she said softly.

He nodded and strode past her into the house, to kneel in front of the chair where Ahava was resting. Leah followed and stood watching them, and she was moved to tears by the tenderness in Tobiah's face as he looked at his grandmother. She held out her arms to him and he allowed her hold him close. After a moment or two he freed himself and got up from the floor. Ahava lent back in her chair, her eyes never leaving his face.

'Don't worry about me, grandmother,' he said. 'My heart isn't broken.'

Ahava shook her head. 'Miriam is a wicked, girl Tobiah. She had us all deceived.'

Leah closed her eyes and a deep feeling of sadness washed over her. How quick we are to condemn others and forget the enormity of what we too are capable of, she thought, as she went to the corner of the room where the empty water jars rested.

As she lifted one down it scraped on the shelf. Tobiah stared at her, almost as though he had forgotten her presence, then he turned back to his grandmother.

'I'm pleased that you and Leah have made your peace with each other,' he said, his voice deep with a resonance she had not heard before. 'You have got back the daughter you thought never to see again, and I have the pleasure of an aunt I knew nothing of.'

He looked from his grandmother to Leah and the expression in his eyes was unfathomable in the dim light of the room. As Ahava passed a warning glance towards her, Leah saw that he had noticed.

'I'll leave you in peace to talk, whilst I go to the well and draw water,' she said. Avoiding looking at either of them she left the room.

Chapter Twenty-Two

It was almost mid-day and Leah knew that the well would be deserted; the women from the village having returned some hours ago after exhausting their excited gossip. She frowned as she walked, thinking of the rumours that would be spreading like fire throughout the village, and she felt a deep concern for Esther. Until now life had been kind to her. She had been blessed with a husband who loved her, two strong sons and clutch of grandchildren. And of course Miriam, who by her betrothal to Tobiah had made her the envy of every mother in Sychar with marriageable daughters.

Now, all the fine plans she and Malachi had begun to make had turned to ashes and they were going to have to bear the disgrace of what their daughter had done. They would both be only too aware of the spiteful gloating of some of their neighbours, even as they expressed their sorrow for what had befallen them. Yet she knew Esther would gladly bear all the disgrace if she could only have Miriam back safely. The pity was that all the pain could have been so easily avoided.

Esther, she was certain, would have begged and cajoled Malachi into allowing Miriam and Caleb to marry, if only the selfish, wilful girl had confessed her love for him before becoming betrothed to Tobiah. But instead Miriam had brought about a trail of grief that had left her father half mad with shame, and her mother broken by her disappearance and the unbearable fear she might be found and stoned to death.

Deep in these thoughts she had reached the well before she became aware of the man sitting there. He appeared to be a Galilean by his looks and almost as though he might be waiting for her. And yet that was not possible. The sun was in the mid-heaven, casting no shadows, and there was no breeze. Her heartbeat quickened because instinctively she knew who he was. Carefully she put her water jar and cup on the ground and looked into the eyes of Jesus, the rabbi that Varinius had spoken so passionately about.

He asked her for a drink, as he had no cup of his own, and her confusion deepened. It was inconceivable that a Jewish rabbi would speak to a woman who was out alone. Surely he must consider it unclean, she thought, to ask for a drink from the cup of a despised Samaritan.

She remained where she was, unmoving, her fists clenched at her sides as she struggled to collect her thoughts. She drew a deep breath and moved closer. Before she could stop herself she had answered him in a tone that was hostile and sharp, demanding to know why he, a Jew, was asking her, a Samaritan, for a drink of water. He took no offence.

He knew about her and all that she had ever done. She asked if he was a prophet but he didn't answer. Instead he engaged her in a conversation that invited her response, treating her, not as an inferior woman incapable of debate, but as a person of substance whose opinion was worthy of attention. As her mind grappled with the strangeness of it all she found herself responding to him with the deepest questions of her heart.

Their conversation sparkled as he challenged her knowledge of scripture, and of the religious conflict that existed between Jews and Samaritans. And she could hardly believe what was happening. Gently he led her towards a new understanding of God's will until, finally, she made a challenge of her own, stating her belief in the coming of the Messiah. It was then he told her that it was he, who was speaking to her.

Before she had time to respond his companions returned from buying food in the village and she saw the astonishment on their faces at discovering him talking with a woman. Although none asked why he was standing with her or what they had been speaking about.

Reluctantly she took her leave of him. As she walked away the words of Varinius echoed in her mind: 'He knew me and he did not judge me.' Well, he had known everything about her too and he had not judged her either. He had treated her with gentleness, compassion and understanding.

As Leah arrived back at her mother's home Tobiah was emerging from the doorway, his head bowed, and she felt fear clutch at her. He looked up as he sensed her presence and there was a deep sadness etched across his face.

'I'm glad you've returned. Grandmother became ill shortly after you left and I think she may be nearing her end. Her breathing is difficult and she is very weak.' He looked at her helplessly. 'She keeps asking for Malachi. She wants to see him.'

Leah raised a hand to her mouth and shook her head. Then, as though it was the most natural thing for him to do, he took her in his arms and she laid her head on his shoulder. As they drew apart she knew that whatever the future held for her, she would always have that moment of comfort from her son to remember.

'I must go to her, Tobiah. She shouldn't be alone.'

'She isn't alone. Esther is with her. She came about an hour ago. She said Malachi and their sons had searched until dark yesterday for Miriam and Caleb, but no one appears to have seen any sign of them. When he arrived back home he said he had given up hope, but then he went out alone at sunrise this morning and he hasn't been back since. I am going to look for him now.'

Unselfconsciously Leah brushed away the wetness of tears from her face and her forehead knotted into a frown of concentration.

'Tobiah, have you heard about a rabbi from Nazareth in Galilee, called Jesus?'

For a moment he appeared startled and then a guarded look crossed his face.

'Yes, I have. There was talk of him in Sebaste when I was there. Some Greeks, who were in the city on business, had heard him preaching when they were travelling through Judea. Why on earth are you asking me about him now?'

'Because I have just met him and his companions at the well.'

It took a moment for him to comprehend what she was saying. He opened his mouth to speak but no words came and his eyes grew round with surprise that a Jewish rabbi should be in Samaria.

'I thought at first he was a prophet and then he told me he was the Messiah we have been waiting for.' She spoke softly and persuasively about her meeting with him.

Tobiah shook his head. 'I have heard some wonderful things about him, but not that he claims to be the Messiah. Are you sure, Leah, that it was the Galilean, that you were speaking to.'

'Yes,' she said simply.

He stood with his head lowered, scratching in the dry earth with the staff he was carrying. When he spoke his voice held a cautious note.

'I don't know what he is doing in Samaria but before I go in search of Malachi I'll get some of the men to go to the well. If he and his companions are still there they can invite them to take lodgings in the village and break bread with us.' A look of bewilderment crossed his face. 'But really, Leah, I can't imagine any Jewish rabbi agreeing to stay amongst Samaritans'

'I think that he will because there is something he needs us to understand' she said softly.

Tobiah stared at her for a moment and then he straightened his shoulders purposefully.

'Go in the house now, Leah. Your mother needs you and so does Esther. If I don't find Malachi within the hour I'll come back.'

As he walked away Leah stood for a moment on the threshold of the mother's home, breathing deeply. With a heavy heart she crossed the floor towards the bedroom and paused in the doorway. Esther was sitting at the foot of Ahava's bed staring straight ahead, her hands folded in her lap. Although the room was dimly lit Leah could see, that even in so short a time, her face bore the marks of a grief that had aged her beyond her years.

She went to the side of the bed and looked down on the small, still frame of her mother, propped up with pillows and covered by a woollen shawl. Her breathing was rapid and shallow and she silently willed her to live until Malachi could be found. As she turned and looked at Esther their eyes locked, and for a long moment neither woman spoke, then Esther signalled towards a stool in the corner of the room.

'Bring that stool and sit beside me, Leah. If Ahava wakes she will want to see you.'

'What happened to her?' she asked, as she sat down. 'I know she is old and frail but she was talking to Tobiah and seemed in good spirits when I left to go to the well.'

'I don't know. It was just as I arrived. As I came through the door she stood up and held out her arms to me, then her face paled and she swayed on her feet. Tobiah caught her before she fell to the ground and carried her to her bed. We thought she was going to die then, but after a while she opened her eyes and asked for you and Malachi. I told her you that wouldn't be long, but that I had not seen Malachi since daybreak and didn't know where he was. She hasn't spoken since.'

Her body shook with harsh dry sobs and she felt the last thin threads of her sanity tighten to snapping point. She fumbled for Leah's hand and clutched it tightly in hers.

'Oh Leah! I love Ahava as I loved my own mother. To lose her now after all that has happened is more than I can bear. This is something else Miriam is responsible for.'

'Try not to worry, Esther, everything will be all right,' Lea said, with a forced brightness. And even before the hollow words of comfort had left her lips she recognised the absurdity of what she was saying.

Esther released her grip and slumped back into her chair, her eyes wide and unfocused.

'I need to go home and wait for Malachi in case he comes back to the house and finds it empty,' she muttered, sitting up straight.

Leah nodded without speaking. As Esther disappeared through the doorway she bent over her mother and laid a hand on her cheek. Ahava's eyes opened and her voice was no more than a fragile whisper as she spoke.

'My heart aches for you Leah. Tobiah told me how you came to be living in his home and what you and your son, Daniel, suffered at the hands of the Roman. Now, I need you to tell me who Daniel's father was and what happened to you after you went to live in Caesarea with Malachi's brother and his wife.'

Leah took her mother's hand in hers and remained silent for a long while.

'I will tell you,' she said finally. 'But my story didn't begin in Caesarea. It began the day I left Sychar with Samuel and Mary. And I must warn you, there is a great deal you will find shameful in what I have done.'

'I don't have the right to judge you or anyone else,' Ahava said, as her eyes closed again.

Leah took a deep breath and began to tell her mother her story.

Chapter Twenty-Three

From the moment Malachi introduced me to Samuel and Mary I knew I would be safe with them. Mary took me to her heart and Samuel, with his quiet gentleness was deeply comforting, although he spoke very little.

When the three of us set off that summer morning, Mary and I were crushed into their little cart, along with their few possessions, and Samuel was leading the donkey.

As you know, we were going to live with Samuel and Malachi's eldest brother, Noah, who had lost his wife in childbirth and was raising six young children alone. Mary could hardly contain her excitement. She had been childless for so long and now she was going to have a brood to care for. I was to help her with the housework and the children whilst Samuel worked alongside his brother at the harbour, loading and unloading the ships. But first we were going to Sebaste to spend some time with Mary's sister Rachael and her family.

Mary held me in her arms as we travelled and cried with me for Tobiah, and I wanted her never to let me go. She said I should have brought him with me, that one more child would have made no difference. But I knew I'd done the right thing in leaving him with Judith and Thomas. They would love and care for him and his future would be assured, because Thomas would teach him his craft as a potter. Not for one moment did I imagine Joseph would leave the farm to him. I thought he would see him as an abomination.

I was sure my husband wouldn't come to the village looking for Tobiah and me but, if he did, I knew Malachi and Thomas would chase him off. The one thing that I was absolutely certain of was that neither you nor Joseph would ever tell anyone who Tobiah's real father was. I consoled myself with that thought.

We stopped several times for rest along the way and it was late afternoon when we arrived in Sebaste. Mary's brother-in-law, Ibsam, was waiting for us just inside the gate. I had never been to the city before and I felt overawed by the sights, sounds, and smells that swept over me. Everywhere there was a riot of noise and bustle.

Mary chattered all the while, clutching at my hand and pinching my arm in order to draw my attention to something she had seen. Samuel said very little, although his eyes were taking everything in. And Ibsam laughed at us, not unkindly, as he chivvied us along until finally we reached his home.

Inside the house Rachael, and her two sons Ulam and Joshua, were waiting to greet us. Ulam, the youngest, was small and slight of build and one of his legs was a bit shorter than the other, causing him to limp awkwardly. He was quietly spoken and I had to lean towards him in order to catch what he said as he greeted me. I knew, from what Mary had proudly told me, that he was a lawyer and a scholar and that he could read and write in Hebrew, Greek and Latin. Joshua was a carpenter, like his father, and he had the same broad shoulders and open, handsome face. His voice was rich and deep and he filled the room with a presence that completely overshadowed his younger brother.

I felt his eyes travelling over my body and then they fixed on mine. There was such admiration in his look that my heartbeat quickened. I became disturbed and frightened then by the strange feeling of excitement he aroused in me, and I had to look away. When I calmed I noticed Ulum staring at his brother and I was shocked by the dark, angry look he was giving him.

Rachael wasted no time in offering towels and water to wash away the dust from our journey and bringing fresh clothes for us to wear. She was a pretty, dainty woman with black, merry eyes and a face that seemed never to have known a days sorrow. As she bustled about preparing supper she directed a constant stream of questions at Mary, not waiting for an answer before rushing on to ask another. And all over Mary's beaming face I could see the love that she had for her sister. I thought of Judith and Tobiah and I cried inside for my sister and my son.

A little while later Ulum excused himself and left, saying that he would be back in time to eat with us. Samuel went to tip out a bag of hay for his donkey, leaving Ibsam and Joshua deep in conversation about the carving of furniture. Their trade had some standing in the city and I knew from what Mary had told me that their business was flourishing.

It had been a long and tiring day and I was sitting in a corner of the room, drifting towards sleep, when I heard Ibsam say something about a marriage contract. My heart started to pound in my chest and I strained to hear their conversation as I watched them through the slits of my eyes.

It soon became clear that Joshua was to be betrothed to the daughter of Ibsam's friend and my eyes snapped wide open. The sharp feeling of disappointment that surged through me left me shocked and bewildered. Ibsam bent to retrieve something from the floor and Joshua turned his head to look at me. He stared and smiled as though he knew what I had been thinking. I realised then I must put all thoughts of him from me.

Two weeks later I was alone in the house. Mary and Rachel had gone to the market to buy food, Joshua, Ibsam and Samuel were at the carpentry shop and Ulum was about his business.

Despite my well-intentioned attempts to ignore Joshua I had not been able to, and now my head was bursting with thoughts of him. From the day we arrived he had not stopped giving me admiring glances. I would feel his eyes on my body whenever he thought no one was looking and then they would meet and hold mine, until I could hardly breathe or look away. Sometimes he brushed against me, as though by accident and then he would let his hand rest briefly on me, hot through the fabric of my tunic. Each time it happened I became overwhelmed with emotions I couldn't understand and that frightened me, and yet I longed to reach up and touch his face with my fingers. He would smile then because he knew.

Never had I known such bitter-sweetness. The way in which he filled my mind aroused in me a longing and a passion I scarcely understood. But I knew that it was wrong and sinful. And yet it eased the loss of losing my son, because whilst I was dreaming of Joshua I was able to blot out the pain of knowing I would never see Tobiah again.

On that morning I made up my mind to put all thoughts of him from me. I promised myself that when next I felt his eyes on me I wouldn't return his look. Instead I would force myself to concentrate on how fortunate I was to have the protection of Mary and Samuel and the promise of our new together life in Caesarea. My good intentions were not to last.

I had lit the oven earlier and was beginning to prepare the bread we would eat with our evening meal, when Joshua came through the open doorway. My stomach churned as I caught sight of him out of the corner of my eye, and my hands shook as I turned away to place the dough on a tray.

Although I deliberately remained with my back towards him, I could feel him silently watching me and I thought my legs would give way. Then my face began to burn and my body trembled as I heard him move a step or two towards me. I was in a confusion of desire and panic, unable to move or speak, just aching to know the feel of his arms around me. To my shame I no longer cared about the girl he was to be betrothed to. He moved closer until I could feel his breath on the back of my neck. My heart was thumping so hard in my breast I was sure he could hear it.

Just as I thought I could bear it no longer he put his hands on my shoulders and turned me round to face him. The power of his look held me spellbound and I felt my face becoming hot. I couldn't turn away and for what seemed an eternity we remained unmoving. As I continued to hold his gaze, I recognised in his eyes the same desire that I knew was burning in mine. My hand shook as I tentatively reached up to trace the contours of his face with my fingers. He bent his head and brushed my lips gently with his. Then he pulled me closer, until out mouths were crushed together. As we drew apart I heard him whisper that I was the most beautiful girl he had ever seen. He lifted me into his arms and said he wanted me to belong to him and I had no strength left to resist. I was overwhelmed that he was declaring his love for me.

As we lay together afterwards I felt happy and at peace as I curled into him. I had only ever known the brutal rape I'd suffered at the hands of my brother and the sick fumbling of old men. To be loved, like that, by Joshua, made me feel clean and whole again.

Shyly I asked if there would be a lot of trouble when he told his parents he wouldn't now be marrying the girl they had chosen for him. He looked at me in amazement and laughed, loudly. He said he had every intention of marrying her. There was menace in his voice as well as panic as he told me I must never tell anyone what had happened between us. He left the house without giving me another glance or word.

For a long while I sat, numbed with shame, hearing the echoes of his laughter in my head until I thought it would burst. My humiliation was more than I could bear. It was now impossible for me to remain in the home of Rachel and Ibsam and I knew I must leave before anyone else returned.

As I began to gather my few belongings together Ulum came through the door, his wide smile quickly fading. Carefully he placed the papers he was carrying onto the table. He had seen at a glance that something was wrong and he asked me quietly what it was. His gentle, brown eyes were filled with such concern that I couldn't look at him. In shame I turned my head and mumbled it was nothing, that I was just feeling a little unwell.

He poured out a cup of water and handed it to me, telling me to sit down and drink. It tasted like vinegar in my mouth, but I sipped at it until it was finished and then I began to sob. Ulum knelt on one knee in front of me and gently lifted my chin to wipe away my tears. He asked if Joshua had been home and I squeezed my eyes shut and clenched my teeth to stop myself from shaking.

It took a while before I could muster the courage to look at him and when I did I saw pity as well as anger in his face. I nodded my head and he bit down on his lip. He said he could guess what had happened between us, because he knew his brother well. I expected him to rebuke me but he didn't. Without raising his voice he told me what had taken place between Joshua and me could not be undone but that I must recognise my share of the blame, however painful that was.

Suddenly, despite his small stature and limp, he seemed so much bigger, so much manlier than his brother. I couldn't bear his knowledge of what had happened and I began to cry again. In a voice that didn't seem to be my own I told him I knew Joshua was about to be betrothed and, between sobs, I kept repeating that I was truly ashamed.

Ulum remained silent for a long while and I waited, dreading what might be coming. I was shocked when he finally spoke. He said he knew a little of my story because he had overheard Mary talking to his mother and so had his brother. His face flushed with anger as he said his brother had taken advantage of my vulnerability, and it was not the first time he had done that sort of thing. There had been many times when he had been forced to rescue him from the wrath of fathers and brothers.

He gave a harsh, humourless laugh and his voice took on a bitter edge. He said he never ceased to be surprised by how a purse full of money could sooth moral outrage. And how fortunate it was he could afford to come to Joshua's rescue when he got into trouble, because his work paid him well and he had neither wife nor child to support.

I felt sick with shame and remorse and I was unable to look at him.

After a moment or two he took my hands in his and told me not to worry because he would take care of everything; I was a guest in his parent's home and this time Joshua had gone too far.

He sat down at the table and put his head in his hands. It was a long time before he looked up and when he did I held my breath. Gently he said that what had happened between Joshua and me must remain a secret. Not for his brother's sake, but for mine and his parents. I couldn't believe what I was hearing when he told me that whatever mess Joshua got himself into in the future he would have to deal with it himself, because he was going to Caesarea with Samuel, Mary and me. He tried to smile but his voice broke as he said it was a thriving city and his skills as a lawyer would be much in demand, and the time had come for him to leave home and make a life for himself away from his brother.

Quickly he gathered up his papers and tucked them under his arm, and then he took my chin with his free hand and smiled at me. It was the sweetest smile I had ever seen. And although I did not deserve it I felt safe. He promised that Joshua would never bother me again and I believed him. Somehow, I managed to stammer my thanks.

At supper that evening Ulum told his parents what he was planning. His mother cried and his father tried hard to dissuade him. Joshua was sullen and subdued and I guessed then that Ulum had already spoken to him. Not once, during the course of that evening, did he look in my direction.

Of course Mary was delighted to have her nephew travel with us, and so too was Samuel, although they both struggled hard not to let it show in front of Rachael and Ibsam. For a brief moment I allowed my eyes to rest on Joshua and I felt a bitter satisfaction, because he was looking so distraught at losing his brother. I wondered how long it would be before he was deep in trouble, with no one to rescue him. And my heart was filled with spite as I hoped it would be soon.

From then on the household became busy with preparations for our journey. Ulum's usually pale cheeks developed a flush of excitement as he bustled about getting his affairs in order. The high esteem in which he was held was clear from the number of the city dignitaries who came to say goodbye and wish him well.

By the end of the week, when we were ready to leave, Joshua was nowhere to be seen and I was grateful for that. Amid much kissing and crying between Mary and her sister we finally set off, with Ulum taking charge of our little party.

For safety we joined up with a trading caravan that was also travelling to Caesarea. Late that afternoon we stopped at a hostelry where the animals could be fed and watered and where we too could wash away the dust of the journey and enjoy a meal.

Ulum busied himself arranging our lodgings for the night and I noticed how, despite his limp and smallness of stature, he commanded respect. Two merchants, who had discovered his profession, came after supper to seek his advice about a legal matter and to ask him to translate a document for them that was written in Latin. He did it with good humour, refusing to take payment. When I asked him about this later he winked at me and said he was building up future business on goodwill, and we laughed together.

The next day, when we reached the home of Samuel and Malachi's eldest brother Noah, he and the children rushed out to great us. Mary's face was red with excitement as she pulled first one child and then another into her arms. Samuel and Noah clasped each other about the shoulders both talking at once. That was the first time I had seen Samuel animated. Ulum and I stood quietly in the background until Mary dragged us both forward into the middle of it all.

Although Noah's house was larger than most, we were still quite overcrowded with six children and four adults, but we soon settled in. The busy streets of the Samaritan quarter had a lively sense of community and it wasn't long before Mary began making friends with the other women and urging me to do the same. Noah had arranged work for Samuel at the harbour and Ulum had found a house nearby and was getting his business established. The traders had spread the word as he hoped they would. I was kept busy all day washing clothes, preparing meals and helping Mary with the children.

A month later I began to feel unwell and each morning I was sick. I knew immediately that I was with child. Mary guessed and, straight away, assumed the baby was my husband's. She could not have been kinder. She held me close and told me that everything would be all right, that it would be another beautiful child to care for. She said I wasn't to worry because Noah and Samuel had plenty of work and there would be enough money. I had never felt more wretched because I knew that the baby was not my husband's.

That night, after supper, I slipped out of the house and went to see Ulum. I owed it to him to let him know I was going away. I had no plan. I just knew I couldn't live a lie and take advantage of Mary and Samuel's kindness after what I had done.

Ulum greeted me warmly, smiling with pleasure because I had come to visit him. The look in his eyes betrayed his feelings for me as it always did and I had to turn my head away. Ever sensitive to my emotions he had guessed immediately that something was wrong and I could see his anxiety as he asked me what it was.

For a moment I was unable speak, then I took a deep breath and told him quickly that I was to have a child and that it was Joshua's. I said I couldn't go on deceiving Samuel and Mary and that I would leave Noah's home and find work until the baby came, or beg in the streets if I had to.

Ulum quickly regained his composure and became the man I had come to know so well. He told me in a voice that brooked no argument he would not allow me to run away, because it would break Mary and Samuel's hearts. And that I wasn't thinking clearly if I thought I would survive alone in a seaport city like Caesarea. Gently he took me by my shoulders and asked me to marry him. He said I was the most beautiful woman he had ever seen, and that he had loved me from the first moment he saw me, although he accepted I could never love him in the same way.

I tried to say that I did love him, but he put a finger on my lips. He said he was taking advantage of my situation but, if I would allow him, he would take care of the baby and me when it was born. There was a tremor in his voice as he reminded me that he was, after all, going to be the child's uncle. Although tears were pouring down my cheeks, and I was suffering a deluge of emotions that were rendering me almost incapable of speech, I managed to stammer that I would marry him.

Ulum then arranged for a messenger to go to my husband's village and offer him a substantial sum of money to divorce me. He said, from what I had told him about Eli, he was sure he wouldn't have any hesitation in accepting the money. Of course he was right.

Two months later we were married. Never had I felt so loved and cherished. Yet I longed for Tobiah and in the dark hours of the night, when I was unable to sleep, I would find myself tormented by thoughts of him and I would despair.

I also felt guilty that I had deceived Ulum by allowing him to believe Tobiah was the son of my husband, and that I had been married only once, not twice. In those seemingly endless nights I would become determined to tell him the whole truth about me, only to lose courage and bury the memories again when morning came. But there is only so long that we can live a lie before the spirit breaks. Daily I became more and more despairing and silent.

Late one afternoon, after we had been married for about six weeks, I was preparing supper when Ulum came in. He stood silently watching me and his expression was the most serious I had ever seen. I began to feel nervous, and when he said he needed to talk to me, my heart started beating so fast I thought it would burst from my chest.

It seemed an age before he spoke again and when he did his voice was grave. He said he knew I must be grieving for the son I had left in Sychar, with my sister, but was sure there was something else troubling me. He asked if I regretted marrying him and was I yearning for his brother. I broke into wild sobs, shaking my head and screaming that I hated Joshua. My body was trembling so much I could hardly stand. In despair I said I loved him, but I was not worthy of him.

Eventually my sobbing subsided, but my legs would no longer hold me and I collapsed onto the floor. Ulum lowered himself down next to me and took me in his arms and his face was grey with shock.

His voice, though, was gentle and kind as he asked if I could tell him what was worrying me. Heartbreakingly he said that whatever it was it would make to difference to his love for me. And so I told him everything that had happened to me from the time my brother raped me to the day I left Sychar with Mary and Samuel. I was weeping uncontrollably when I said the only people to know the truth about Tobiah's conception were my mother and father, because Reuben was dead.

For a long while Ulum sat with his head in his hands, until finally I could stand it no longer. I shouted at him to say something. He stood up slowly and without looking at me he left the house.

I don't know how many hours passed but daylight had faded and I was still sitting where he had left me when he returned. Without speaking he lit the lamps and poured himself a cup of wine, which he drained before turning to look at me. There was no anger, only sorrow in his face. I held my breath, certain he was about to tell me he was divorcing me and that I must leave his home. But he didn't. Instead he gathered me to him and wept. He stroked my hair and said that my suffering had been great and that he loved me dearly.

What he proposed next shocked me even more. We were to go to Sychar and tell my sister that I was now able to provide for Tobiah, and we would bring him to our home where he could grow up with the baby that I was expecting.

I could hardly believe what I was hearing and I vowed then that I would love and care for Ulum, with every fibre of my being, until the day I died. But the pain I knew I was going to inflict on my sister, when I took Tobiah from her, tempered my joy.

When Ulum said we would be going first to Sebaste, because he wanted to see his parents, I was filled with apprehension at the thought of meeting Joshua again. He told me not to worry because it was not yet obvious I was with child and he would ensure he kept his distance from me.

Two weeks later we set off. Ulum had told Samuel and Mary that we were going for Tobiah and that he would be proud to be a father to him. They were waiting in their doorway to wish us a safe journey and Mary's eyes danced with joy as she took me in her arms. She whispered in my ear how happy she was for me, and Samuel's face was wreathed in smiles as he waved us off. That was the last time I ever saw them.

By the time we reached the coastal road the sun was warming the air. It was unusually quiet of traffic and for the first half-mile we met only two small caravans of camels and a troop of Roman soldiers, clanking their way to Caesarea.

After an hour we left the road and joined one of the trading routes, crossing the Plain of Sharon that would take us to Sebaste. Ulum walked close beside me, guiding me with one hand around my waist, the other holding the reins of the donkey that was loaded with food and water for our journey, and a change of clothes for when we arrived. There was also a small wooden horse for Tobiah, that Ulum had spent many hours carving, and presents for Judith, Thomas and his parents.

We talked softly together in whispers, almost as though fearful we might be overheard, although there was no one else to be seen. After a while Ulum brought the donkey to a halt and drew me to him. I bent my body gladly towards him, savouring the preciousness of the moment and anticipating the joy that was to come when I was reunited with my son.

As we pulled apart, smiling foolishly at each other, a cloud passed over the sun and I felt a chill, even though there was no breeze. I heard Ulum take a sharp intake of breath and I followed his gaze.

Riding towards us, with swords raised high, were two men on horseback. It didn't last long. As the front rider reached us he brought his sword flashing down, almost severing Ulum's neck. His blood spurted high into the air and sprayed over me. For an indescribable moment he remained standing and then he fell to the ground. By then both riders were circling me and I fainted.

When I recovered one of the men lifted me onto his horse and mounted up behind me. I twisted my head around as far as I could and looked back at Ulum. I saw the man who had killed him aiming a vicious kick at his body. He then began unloading our donkey, putting the presents we had bought and Ulum's money pouch into his own bag. Then I heard someone screaming. It was only when the man behind me put his over my mouth that I realised it was me.

I don't remember much about the journey that followed, or in which direction we travelled, just the steady thud of hooves. After what seemed like hours we stopped and I was lifted down and offered water and a small loaf of bread. I drank the water but refused to eat. I also kept my eyes averted from the men who had captured me. I knew they were slave kidnappers and that an uncertain fate awaited me and I wept silently for the child in my womb and for Ulum.

The sun was at its highest point as we set off again, and dipping below the horizon in the west when we arrived at our destination. I was lifted from the horse and hoisted onto the shoulder of the rider.

Although my eyes were swollen with crying, I saw we were in a valley surrounded by hills. Hedgerows were separating the fields of waving grain and a small group of houses clustered close by.

Suddenly the whole place erupted with noise and movement. Women emerged from open doorways and a small boy and girl ran towards us, scattering the squawking, fluttering chickens that had been peacefully pecking in the dust. From somewhere far off I heard the bleating of sheep.

Two of the younger women were holding babies in their arms and all were calling a welcome to the men who had murdered my husband. An older boy appeared and ran to take the reins of the horse. The man holding me shifted my weight higher on his shoulder. My stomach contracted and I screamed and writhed as I felt the wet, sticky warmth of blood between my legs. He shouted a woman's name, calling for her to come quickly, as he let me slide to the ground.

There was a shocked hush and then the sound of urgent whisperings as the children were ushered away. I was incapable of making any effort to resist as he lifted me again in his arms and carried me into one of the houses, laying me on a cot. I screamed then, as I was gripped by a spasm so strong that I became oblivious to everything around me.

As the pain subsided I lay with my eyes closed thinking that I had been left alone. When a hand was placed on my head I cried out in terror and the hand was quickly removed. I peered up and in the dim light of the room I could just make out the small slender figure of an elderly woman. Without speaking she began trimming the wick of a lamp and lighting it. Its glow only just illuminated the corner where I lay.

The next few hours were a blur of agony until finally it was over. I had lost my baby. The woman, who had remained with me throughout, put an arm under my shoulders and helped me to sit up. She held a cup to my lips and in a deep, gentle voice she said I must drink and it would ease the pain and help me sleep. I did as she asked.

The taste was bitter and I choked as the liquid trickled down my throat but she kept on pouring. When it was finished I slid back down onto the cot and lay there, still as stone, staring up at her. The expression on her face was unfathomable in the gloom. She covered me with a blanket and after a while my eyes grew heavy. As I drifted towards the blessed relief of sleep I wondered who she was.

When I awoke the lamp had gone out and the room was in darkness, except for a thin shaft of sunlight filtering through a crack in the wooden shutter covering the window. I don't know for how long I lay there, or what time of day it was. My senses were so numbed I felt neither the pain of losing my child, nor anguish for Ulum. There was just the cold certainty that I would end my life as soon as I could find the means.

After what seemed like endless hours I heard the door open and the same woman entered the room. I stayed as still as I could so she wouldn't guess that I was awake. But I watched her, through half closed eyes, as she carried the pile of clean linen and the bowl of water she was holding, to a table by the window. Carefully she dragged it across the room making sure the water didn't slop over the sides of the bowl. Absurdly I found myself thinking it would have been easier for her if she had placed the bowl and the linen by my cot and then carried the table across.

She closed the door and opened the window shutters and sunlight streamed through. I could feel her eyes on me as she walked back to where I lay. Brusquely she said she had come to help me wash and then, more kindly, she asked if I realised that I had lost the child I had been carrying. I turned my head away without answering and submitted to her.

She bathed me gently. When it was done she gave me a fresh pad of linen to put between my legs to staunch the flow of blood and slipped a clean, loose fitting tunic over my head. Afterwards she took a brush to my hair. Despite my determination to take no comfort from her, I found the long rhythmic strokes soothing. When she had finished she stood looking down at me, and her lips moved as though there was something she wanted to say. Instead, in silence, she filled a cup from the water jug and held it whilst I drank. It tasted as sweet as honey and I hated myself for enjoying it, because Ulum was dead.

I watched as she busily gathered up the soiled linen, putting it into the bowl she was holding against her hip. And then she spoke. She told me her name was Talitha and that she was going to prepare me some food. She hitched the bowl higher and asked my name. I turned my head from her and closed my eyes. She left then, quietly closing the door behind her.

Some time later she returned with a dish of corn porridge and told me that I must eat. But I pushed it away. I learned from her that I was in the home of her son, Saul, a slave trader, who would want to see me as soon as I had recovered. She said I was to be taken by ship to Ephesus, where I would be sold privately to a wealthy Roman, who was a friend of her son. He and his partners would then buy more slaves from the wholesaler at the emporium, and sell them at auctions throughout Palestine.

I mustered as much venom as I could and spat out that the selling of slaves legally was one thing, but the murder and kidnap of innocent travellers was a criminal act, and I hoped the Roman authorities would discover their illegal activities and hang them from wooden crosses. She was quick to say it was her son's partners who had committed those crimes, not him. I snapped back that he was still prepared to profit from my sale. The anguish that appeared on her face surprised me and I felt my anger with her die.

The days and nights that followed blurred into one, as I lay on that small cot inert with grief. Talitha spent many hours coaxing me into eating the delicacies she had prepared, and rubbing sweet smelling oils into my skin and brushing my hair until it shone.

She was curious about me and she probed and questioned but I stubbornly refused to answer. In the end she wore me down by her persistence. I said the only thing I was prepared to tell her was that my husband had been an educated man and a lawyer, and that I had loved him dearly, and no man could ever replace him in my heart.

She looked at me as if she couldn't believe what she was hearing. Then she opened her mouth to speak and closed it again, at a loss for words. I guessed then that she had been told about Ulum's deformed leg and small stature.

I was shaking with rage as I screamed at her that without my husband my life was no longer worth living, and I would find a way to end it. Then I howled and wailed. She stayed with me until I had sobbed myself into a state of exhaustion.

As my strength returned I spent my days fantasising about plunging a dagger into the stomach of Ulum's murderer and watching him die, writhing in agony, as I twisted it. At night I tossed and turned brooding on how, once aboard the ship, I could escape my captors and throw myself into the sea.

I made up my mind to tell Talitha I was well enough to be taken to her son. I knew she would be upset because she had grown fond of me and would be reluctant to admit the time had come. She had treated me tenderly and sometimes she had even managed to make me laugh. I wanted to hate her because she was my captor's mother, but I couldn't. In fact, in the strange half-life I was leading in that small room, I had become fond of her too.

As she stood over me the next day, brushing my hair and chattering excitedly about a new garment she was making for me to wear, I interrupted her. I said if I was to be sold into slavery, I was ready. She put the brush down and took me by my shoulders. Then she cupped my chin and her hand was shaking. She said I was very beautiful and the minute her son saw me he would know he could ask a high price for me. I didn't answer because I knew I would never be sold to anyone. I was going to drown myself first.

She sat down beside me and her eyes filled with tears as she asked if she could tell me about Saul. Childishly I clamped my hands over my ears, shouting I didn't want to hear anything about her son. Then I caught the expression on her face and grudgingly I agreed to listen.

She remained silent for a while, gathering her thoughts. At first her voice was hesitant as she told me how her parents had arranged her marriage to a man from Nazareth, a devout Jew who was hard working and respected by everyone who knew him. She he had fallen in love with him almost at first sight.

Within ten months she had given birth to a daughter. Seventeen years later Saul was born and her husband finally had the son he longed for. By the time he was two their daughter had died in childbirth.

She gave a harsh laugh as she told me their grief was bearable only because of the promise for the future that rested in their beautiful son. Then her mouth trembled and tears poured down her cheeks.

I put my arms around her and held her until she stopped crying. She got up awkwardly then, almost as though her body had become too stiff to move, and filled a cup with water that she sipped at until it was empty.

When she sat down again she took my hand in hers and squeezed it tight, holding it to her breast until I thought my fingers might break. After she released me I remained as still as I could whilst I listened to the rest of her story.

She told me that as Saul grew from childhood to boyhood he became wilful and hard to control. He was always in trouble with their neighbours for some malicious mischief or other, and with the rabbi at the synagogue for refusing to learn scripture. But he feared neither his father nor his uncles, who tried to beat sense into him, and certainly not the Jewish or Roman authorities he felt always able to outwit.

As he grew older the problems got worse. He was now mixing with some of the most disreputable men in Galilee and his wildness and drunken behaviour shamed them before their neighbours.

He had refused to join his father in his trade of tent making, and nor did he do any other work, yet he always had a great deal of money. She and her husband believed he was a thief or worse. They lived with the constant dread that, sooner or later, he would be caught and sentenced to death by crucifixion. Eventually the worry and the disgrace became too much for his father and after a short illness he died.

Her tears flowed again as she said she now had no means of support other that her skills as a midwife and for this she had never charged. To her deep humiliation she was forced to rely on the charity of her neighbours for food and she could hardly bear their pity.

The day Saul came to her door offering her money she turned him away, saying he was no longer her son.

When he came back a year later he was clean and sober and she invited him in, hardly daring to hope her prayers had been answered and that he had finally repented and found reputable work. She was quickly disillusioned.

He and his two friends, Aaron and Yaris, had set up a partnership and obtained licenses to trade in the buying and selling of slaves and he was living with them and their families in the countryside of lower Galilee. He had laughed when he told her it was a remote place and the only people likely to visit were the tax collectors.

She was too afraid to ask where the money had come from to set up this venture because she didn't want to hear the answer.

Saul was very persuasive in begging her to go with him and share his home. He told her he and his partners would be away about their business for many months each year and whilst they were gone the two younger brothers of Yaris would farm the land and look after the women and children.

He pleaded that an older woman, skilled in midwifery as she was, would be of great benefit to their small village. She would be able to befriend the younger women, mediate in their quarrels and help when they, or their children, fell sick. It wasn't until he said she could gain their confidence and act as his eyes and ears, that she realised Saul didn't entirely trust his partners.

She was both angry and saddened to discover the true reason he wanted her to live with him was because he needed her as an ally and a spy. Although she asked him to leave and come back the next day for her answer, she already knew she would go with him.

Despite everything he had done he was still her child, and although she had long ago ceased to like him, she had never stopped loving him.

Once she arrived at her new home it didn't take her long to realise Saul was the leader of this small community and that the other men deferred to his judgements. Although she sensed they too had a deep dislike of him.

He didn't have a wife at that time but two years later, after being away for many months, he had arrived home with a young bride of sixteen. A Phoenician girl named Naomi. In the five years that had passed since then there had been no children. It was clear from the expression on her face, as she told me this that she held her daughter-in-law to blame.

When she said Naomi was as ugly as sin and as fat as a pregnant cow, with the nature of a viper, I had to clamp my hands to my mouth to stop myself from laughing. She was so incensed about her and her failure to conceive she didn't notice my amusement.

With great bitterness she said she often wondered how many grandchildren she might have in the many towns and cities her son had run wild in over the years.

Then, almost as though she regretted what she had been telling me she stood up abruptly and began to bustle about, tidying things.

As I watched her I had an idea about how I might strike back at her son. On the night Samuel, Mary, Ulum and I had taken lodgings at the hostelry, on our journey to Caesarea, I had overheard two Jewish traders talking together. I would use what they had been discussing.

For some reason Talitha had assumed that I was Jewish and I had not told her otherwise. Now I was going to let her continue believing it. I told her to tell her son the enslavement of one Jew by another was a grave sin, because a Jew was already a slave of God.

I didn't expect what happened. She backed away, staring at me, and then she began to cry as though her heart would break. Between sobs she said it would make no difference because Saul had turned his back on God many years ago.

On the following day, before she took me to him, she dressed me in the garment she had just finished making. Afterwards she spent a long time brushing my hair and fussing until I told her to stop.

She seemed agitated and there was a high flush on her cheeks. When I asked her what was wrong her agitation increased. To my horror she said she had begged Saul to pay Aaron and Yaris their share of what I was worth and then allow her to keep me as her companion. He was to make his decision after he had seen me. Too stunned to speak I stared at her, shaking my head vehemently from side to side, knowing my plan to drown myself might be taken from me.

She watched me in silence, biting her lip, and then she drew me to her and began stroking my back. She said she knew what I was planning because she had seen the same black despair in my eyes that she had suffered after her husband had died. Gently she begged me to listen to her, telling me I would not feel that way forever. But I didn't want to hear. I glared and pulled away from her.

Her voice was thick with tears as she said she too had once wanted to turn her face to the wall and die, but life had reclaimed her and it would reclaim me too, if only I would allow it.

As she took me in her arms again I was too grief-stricken to argue. I told her to do with me as she wished, because I had no other choice. But I was determined that if Saul allowed his mother to keep me, I would find another way to kill myself.

She became all bustle and hurry then, adjusting the purple sash she had tied around my waist and once more taking a brush to my hair. She moved a step backwards and stood smiling fondly at me. For a brief moment I allowed the warmth of her affection to wash over me and then I steeled myself against it. But I knew that she had noticed.

Her face clouded when she said it was clear I would bring a large sum and her son had a great love of money. But she had never asked him for anything before and her hope was he would let her keep me.

Without further fuss she placed a veil on my head and gave me a gentle push towards the door. As I emerged from the dimness of the room a cold numbness gripped my body. And something was gnawing at me. I wondered why, if she wanted to keep me, she had taken such trouble over my appearance. It would have been better to ensure I looked as plain as possible. And then I knew. She wanted her son to find me attractive. She despised her ugly, barren daughter-in-law and was hoping he would take me as his concubine and that I would provide her with the grandchildren she longed for.

As she led me to the room where Saul was waiting I kept my eyes lowered and my head bent. He was sitting in a chair by the window and I could feel his eyes raking over me. He told me to lift my head and his voice was deep and soothing, like his mother's. Talitha was gripping my arm at the top and digging her fingers into my flesh. As I looked up at him I felt a jolt of shocked surprise.

He got up slowly from his chair and walked towards me. There was a knowing amusement in his eyes, and the faint trace of a smile at the corners of his mouth. Nothing about him resembled the coarse, vulgar man of my imaginings. He was tall and slim with the face of an angel. Unlike other Jewish men he didn't wear a beard and his black hair, cut short in the Roman style, curled around his ears. His smile widened, revealing even, white teeth.

Talitha let go of my arm and I began to tremble as he took me by my shoulders and drew me to him, inspecting me closely. His hands were delicate, with long tapering fingers, and his nails were clean and cut short. As he released me and stepped back I smelt the sweet perfume of Frankincense. He walked back to his chair and sat down, then he signalled me to come closer.

Reluctantly I moved a few steps towards him and lowered my head, waiting for him to speak. When he did it was not what I expected to hear. He said he was sorry for what his partners had done to my husband, and that his mother had told him Ulum had been a man of education and culture and worked as a lawyer.

His voice was soft and concerned and he smiled, sadly, creases appearing in the corners of his eyes. Once again I was thrown into confusion because he was nothing like the man I had expected to meet. Even so, he didn't deceive me. I knew his real regret was not that Ulum had been brutally killed, but that he had learned from Talitha he was so much more than a frail looking man with a limp, and would have been worth a considerable amount of money for his skills.

I screamed inside and my hands curled. I wanted to gouge his face. He saw my look and in an instant his manner changed. He became distant and dismissive. He stood up and abruptly told Talitha that he was happy to grant her wish. She could keep me. In a state of turmoil I watched him stride from the room.

Talitha was overjoyed. She hugged me to her and whispered in my ear how happy she was that we were not going to be parted. She made no mention of Saul's wife. I was about to ask how Naomi would feel having me living in her home when, as abruptly as he had left Saul returned. He was holding out something in his hand. The breath left my body as I recognised immediately the little horse Ulum had carved so lovingly for Tobiah. I stood looking at it, unable to move. He asked if it had been a present for a child and I grabbed it from him without answering. He nodded to his mother before walking away again.

As I clutched the carving to my breast Talitha took me in her arms and held me in a tight grip until my sobbing subsided. Startled by a hoarse, snorting laugh we pulled apart and there, standing framed in the doorway, glaring at us, was the fattest woman I had ever seen. Her small black eyes, buried deep in the fleshy folds of her face, were filled with hatred and I knew that this was Naomi.

She hissed and said she could see her husband had given me the carving she had wanted. For a moment my senses swam and then I felt a hot, surging anger. I think I would have hit her with it if Talitha had not held on to me. I screamed that it belonged to me, and I almost choked on the bile that was rising in my throat. Naomi smiled, triumphant that she had managed to provoke me. And even in my rage I noticed the gaps in her mouth, where her teeth were missing. As we stood glaring at each other I knew I had made a bitter enemy.

The following day Saul, Aaron and Yaris left for the seaport at Caesarea where they would board a sailing ship to Ephesus. It was to be almost nine months before they returned. Each man had left his family well provided for. There were dried fruits, sacks of grain and jars of oil and wine in the barn, and Yaris's brothers continued to farm the land and look after the women and children.

Life took on a slow, repetitive rhythm and as the months went by my overwhelming grief for the loss of Tobiah, Ulum and my baby began to subside into the dull ache that would never leave me. Slowly my desire to end my life released its grip, to be replaced by a longing to escape and find my way back to Samuel and Mary. How could I have known then that their home had burned down and they had died in the fire?

Eventually I grew accustomed to the existence I was leading and my longing to escape began to fade. What never went away was the hatred I harboured in my heart for Aaron, the man who had murdered Ulum. And in the long, sleepless nights, I would dream up ways to harm him and watch him suffer.

My days were kept busy helping Talitha with the grinding of flour and the many household chores, as well as working in the fields at harvest time. The other women had been hostile at first but slowly they began to accept me, and I forced myself to help with their children.

Naomi was forever pleading headaches and sickness and she managed to do very little, beyond complaining about her aches and pains. She had me constantly dancing attendance on her; calling for me to provide her with something she wanted, or to rub oil into her feet that were swollen and sore because of her great size, which seemed to increase with every passing day. On the few occasions she did emerge from the house the children would make fun of her, running behind her back, pulling faces and mimicking her waddling walk. Their mothers pretended not to notice so they didn't have to scold them.

As the time approached for the men to return the excitement amongst the women and children grew. Naomi begged Talitha to make her a new sash and tunic, her old ones having become much too tight. To the amusement of the other women Talitha said that she now felt qualified to take up the trade of her late husband, a tent maker.

Each day Aaron's youngest daughter climbed to the top of a nearby hill to look out for her father. On the morning that she came running back, waving her arms and shouting that she had seen three riders in the distance, there began a frantic flurry of activity as the women rushed to wash their children, and change into their new clothes.

The men and young boys came in from the fields and a slaughtered lamb was put on a spit to roast. Tables and cushions were carried outside and the best jars of wine brought from the barn. In the midst of all the preparations Talitha remained still and calm. I knew she was offering up a prayer of gratitude that her son had come home safely, and had not been shipwrecked or killed by pirates as he had gone about his business of buying and selling slaves.

All that day feasting and dancing to flutes and tambourines went on until sundown. Then one by one the babies and small children, who had fallen asleep in their mother's arms, were carried to their cots and the celebrations came to an end. Saul had never moved from his seat next to Naomi, who was dressed in the new tunic Talitha had made for her. If he was disgusted by her great size, or the amount of food she had eaten and the wine she had drunk, he didn't let it show.

When almost everyone had retired to bed he too rose from the table and held out his hands to her, heaving her up from the large cushion she had been sitting on. He glanced towards me and there was a dangerous message in the mocking depth of his eyes. My face began to burn and Naomi, who missed nothing when it came to Saul, gave me a look of pure hatred. I knew she was suspicious of me and convinced that I wanted to steal her husband from her.

The following morning, as I helped her dress, I tried to reassure her. I told her that although Saul had not been party to the murder of Ulum I hated him as much as I hated Aaron and Yaris. And as I looked into her blotched and despairing face I swore to myself I would find a way of avoiding him whenever he was home. I redoubled my efforts to befriend her, ashamed that I had laughed with the other women, behind her back. But I was ashamed most of all by what lay treacherous and unspoken between her husband and me.

Of course the decision to avoid Saul was never mine to make. Inevitably, when he was ready, he claimed me. Talitha was delighted but Naomi's trust in me was gone. Saul, however, continued to give her the protection of being his wife and she always had pride of place beside him. But she never spoke to Talitha again because she blamed her for her for her husband's infatuation with me.

I conceived twice over the next three years, each time losing the baby. And then Daniel was born. As Talitha placed him in my arms I was filled with gratitude that I had been given the blessing of another child to love and care for. I had expected him to look like Saul but he didn't, he looked like me. Talitha was beside herself with joy. She could hardly believe her good fortune that she finally had the grandson she so passionately wanted. For hours she would sit nursing him and telling him how beautiful he was.

On the day I found Naomi leaning over Daniel's crib, I braced myself, ready to leap forward and drag her away if she tried to harm him. She sensed my presence and turned her head to look at me. Her face was filled with a look of such unhappiness and longing that, without thinking, I rushed forward and picked up Daniel, thrusting him into her arms. For a long time she stood holding him and looking down into his face. Then she hugged him close and her tears welled and fell, wetting the blanket that covered him. From that moment an uneasy truce developed between us and whenever Saul was away she would ask to nurse Daniel. I think she grew to love him almost as much as I did.

The greatest change was in Saul. From being a boy he had derided his Jewish faith and mocked God, but on the eighth day following the birth of our child he ensured that he was circumcised and given the name of Daniel. When the time came for us to be purified he insisted we make the three-day journey to the Temple in Jerusalem where Daniel would be consecrated to the Lord in keeping with the Law of Moses. He seemed to have forgotten that Naomi was his wife, not I.

Daniel was about eight years old when Saul grew a beard and began to wear his hair longer. When he came home from his travels he would often take lodgings in Nazareth and spend days at the Synagogue, studying scripture and talking with the rabbi. And then he would instruct Daniel.

He also became kinder to Naomi, without my continually having to beg him to pay her attention. He brought her little gifts back from his travels and lotions for her legs and feet, that were now so swollen she could hardly stand. She was pathetically grateful and would thank me, giving me the credit for his kindness. I felt a deep disgrace because I knew she truly loved him, whereas what I felt for him was something shameful.

When Daniel reached twelve Saul told me he was finished with slavery and that we would be going to live in Jerusalem where our son could study at the best school. He said arrangements were already in hand to have a house built there. With the light of zeal in his eyes he told me Daniel would become a man of learning and culture and rise in the world. He shocked me to my core when he said he was going to divorce Naomi because she was not Jewish and because she had never born him a child. I thought it would have been a miracle if she had, because I had never known him lie with her.

When he told me that we would marry after the divorce my heart began to thump in by breast. I knew I had done wrong in allowing him and Talitha to believe that I was Jewish, but I wasn't going to tell them the truth now. My main concern was the welfare of my son, although I did worry for Naomi.

I asked Saul what was to happen to her. He shrugged and said he had only married her for the enormous dowry her father had provided and couldn't tolerate the sight of her any longer. She was to go back to her family.

When I asked if he was going to return her dowry he smiled without answering. Somehow I knew then that his return to his Jewish faith was a sham to further his ambitions. He would keep her dowry because he needed all the money he could raise to give him eminence in Jerusalem, where he would practise as a devout Jew in order to create the life he desired for himself and Daniel. He needed me as his wife to complete the image he was constructing. His little kindnesses to Naomi had been his way of making her grateful to him and compliant with his wishes.

I think he saw in my eyes how much I despised him. His tone became dismissive, as it always did when he found himself challenged and the finality in his manner chilled me. But I tried to plead for Naomi. I reminded him how much she had come to love our child and how much Daniel loved her and I begged him to allow her to stay.

When I talked of the dangers she might encounter on the road his eyes darkened and became hard. I knew then he was thinking about the capture of me and the murder of Ulum. Abruptly he said he would ensure she travelled in comfort and that he would provide guards to protect her on the journey. All of my pleadings fell on deaf ears. He had made up his mind.

That night, after he told Naomi her fate, the sound of crying, coming from her room at the back of the house, was louder than the snores of her husband lying oblivious at my side. Before I could move I heard Daniel get up and go to her. The next morning I found them both asleep together, Daniel was curled into her back with his thin boyish arm thrown across her huge body in comfort. Two weeks later Saul gave her a bill of divorce and she was sent on her way back to her family.

It would be six months before the grand house in Jerusalem was finished. In the meantime, Saul and I were married. Talitha made the wedding robes and no expense was spared on the festivities that went on for days. When Naomi crept into my thoughts I comforted myself that she was better off with her own kin, and I tried to ignore the deep sense of foreboding that had settled on me.

Daniel missed her and asked after her constantly. But as his spirits began to revive he became as excited as his grandmother about our move to Jerusalem. I was unable, though, to shake off my feeling of apprehension.

Talitha laughed and dragged me into her arms when she saw me brooding. She held me tight and told me I was not to be afraid and that I must learn how to be happy. But still the feeling persisted.

As the arrangements for our journey came to completion, and the time approached for us to leave, I began to feel more at ease. Despite reminding myself I didn't deserve to have any contentment, because of what had happened to Naomi, I started to look forward to the future and what it might hold for Daniel.

Two days before we were due to set off on our journey to Jerusalem I was awoken in the night by the raised voices of men shouting commands. As I lay, trying to make sense of what was happening, there came an eerie high-pitched wailing. It took a moment before I realised it was the sound of petrified women and children.

Saul leapt from our bed and was reaching for his sword as Talitha appeared in the doorway. He pushed us both roughly to one side, ordering us to remain where we were. But we didn't, we followed him outside. What met our eyes was a sight of unimaginable carnage. I immediately thought we had been invaded by bandits.

The barn was alight and the screaming of the animals tethered inside split the night air. A group of men, some on horseback and some on camels, were circling the dead bodies of Yaris and his two brothers. Another man was standing guard over the younger boys and girls and the women holding babies in their arms. All had been dragged from their beds and were huddled together in terror.

Then I saw Aaron lying dead on the ground a little way from our door. He must have been coming to warn us. And even in the midst of all that horror I felt glad the man who had murdered Ulum was no longer alive.

In that moment one of the riders broke away from the circling group and made straight for us. Saul didn't have time to raise his sword before his head was severed from his body. Then I saw the killing lust in the eyes of the man who had felled him as he turned on Talitha. His sword was still dripping with the blood of her son as it pierced her breast. As she fell I heard an awful howling noise and I realised that it was coming from me.

Desperate to reach Daniel I tried to run back into the house but the man who had killed Saul and Talitha barred my way. He pulled me towards him and held me in a tight grip, almost lifting me off my feet. Venomously he hissed in my face that he was Naomi's brother and that he had come with his kinsmen to avenge her and take back her dowry. He shook me, fiercely, and demanded to know where Daniel was.

Almost mad with fear for my son I tried to wrest myself from his hold. As we struggled I saw Daniel, out of the corner of my eye, standing transfixed in the doorway. Desperately I signalled him to move away. It was too late. Naomi's brother had already seen him. He threw me to the ground and before I had time to get up he was back, thrusting Daniel, petrified and shaking, down into my arms. Then he stood over us, hatred burning in his eyes.

Spitting out the words he said he would like to have killed us both and forced Saul to watch, but Naomi had pleaded for us to be spared. He laughed then and it was a chilling sound. He said we were both to be sold at a slave auction and he hoped we would be bought by the cruellest of masters. Our hands and feet were tied with rope and we were left lying there whilst he ransacked the house. His grin was triumphant as he reappeared, carrying two heavy moneybags with their seals intact. He had found Naomi's dowry and the money Saul had saved over many years.

I knew it would be a long while before anyone discovered what had happened in our small village, and by the time they did, there would be no one alive to say who had been responsible.

Naomi's revenge on Saul and those who had diminished her by their mockery and laughter was complete.

Two weeks later Daniel and I stood on a dais at a slave auction with our bare feet coated in chalk, enduring the poking and prodding of the auctioneer. As I became aware of a man watching me, I knew from the way his eyes roved over my body, that he was considering buying me. Boldly I met and held his gaze. My only hope for Daniel, who had not spoken since the night of the slaughter, lay in being able to persuade this Roman into buying him too. I couldn't have guessed then the brutality of his nature.

No one outbid the price he offered and I was pushed from the dais. I caught sight of Daniel's face and he was wide-eyed and shaking with fear. With a tilt of my chin I met and held the eyes of the man who had purchased me and smiled. I placed my lips close to his ear and whispered to him to buy the boy. I said he had a wonderful way with horses and could ride as well as any grown man. He would be an asset to his household.

He didn't answer immediately and then he threw his head back and laughed. My limbs trembled as I struggled to keep my composure. I knew, instinctively that this man would not buy Daniel if he thought he meant something to me. I shrugged my shoulders and smiled as he took my arm to lead me away. But my heart was breaking.

We had gone only a few steps when he stopped and signalled a bid to the auctioneer for Daniel, and I held my breath. There was no other interest in him and within moments I was holding his hand. We were to be the slaves of Marcellus for over three years, until we escaped.

Chapter Twenty-Four

As Leah reached the end of her story she lowered her head and with a feeling of utter exhaustion she covered her face with her hands. When she felt her mother touch her arm and heard her voice, small and weak, saying her name, she looked up. She had expected to see shock and condemnation in her eyes. Instead they were filled with a look of love and understanding that enveloped her like a healing balm. As Ahava's fingers curled around hers a deep sense of peace settled between them.

She was unaware of the passage of time until she heard Tobiah's voice behind her. As she turned her head she saw him and Esther framed in the doorway with Malachi behind them. Tobiah strode quickly to his grandmother's bedside and bent to kiss her, and the tears were wet on his cheeks as he stroked her hair. Esther moved to stand next to Leah and held out her hand towards Malachi who had remained in the doorway. For a moment he hesitated then, without looking at her, he walked to the other side of bed. An hour later as they watched over her, Ahava died.

Tenderly, Leah and Esther washed and oiled her body and wrapped her in long strips of fine, white linen, packed with aromatic herbs to take away the pungent smell of death. Candles were lit and prayers were said over her body and then they closed up her house.

In the early morning they took her to the burial place and the tomb where Daniel lay. Tobiah and Malachi walked at the head of her bier, carrying it on their shoulders, whilst Malachi's sons took the weight at the back. In their wake came two pipers, playing a soft lament, followed by Leah, Esther and her daughters-in-law. Then came the men and women of the village banging tambourines and drums. As they wound their way in slow procession the voices of young boys, chanting scripture in the schoolroom of the synagogue, echoed in the narrow street.

Malachi bent his head as he walked, not from the grief of Ahava's death, nor the burden of carrying her slight frame, but instead weighed down by the shame and anger he felt for his daughter's sin, and for the ill concealed pity of his neighbours and friends. He knew too that there were those amongst them whose spirits were mean and spiteful and who would secretly be pleased to see his downfall.

He loved Tobiah like a son. For his daughter to become betrothed to him and then to hurt and shame him was more than he could bear. Consumed with rage and frustration at not being able to find her and have her punished, there was no room left in his heart to grieve for the woman who had been his lifelong friend, and who had shown him nothing but kindness. Nor could he look at Tobiah, who had not said one word in condemnation of Miriam, and who was still prepared to employ him on his land.

Angrily he had forbidden Esther ever to speak their daughter's name again. And she grieved, not just for the loss of Miriam but also for the loss of the husband who had never raised his voice to her before, nor said an unkind word. The thick silence that had lain between them since she had told him what Miriam and Caleb had done, had grown more impenetrable and bitter with each passing hour, until there was no comfort left in their home. Now he longed for the funeral to be over so he could escape and be alone with his pain.

As night fell, and the sky flushed red with the last rays of the dying sun, Tobiah and Leah sat together in mourning for Ahava, each absorbed in their own thoughts and oblivious of the other. On the table in front of them two cups of wine lay untouched.

Tobiah's face was drawn and pale and his hand trembled as he stroked the dog that that had come to his side, pawing gently at his thigh and giving soft yelps. Pulled from out of her reverie by the movement and noise Leah sought to find words of comfort.

'I know how much you loved your grandmother, Tobiah, and how painful her death must be. But we were reconciled before she died and I think it brought her comfort'

'I'm sure it did. But what happened with Miriam caused her great distress. And I must share some of the blame for that.'

His expression was guarded and Leah shook her head.

'You have nothing to reproach yourself for. And you have every right to be angry with Miriam, even though you don't want to see her punished.'

'No I don't. She isn't the only one at fault, Leah. To have her stoned to death would serve no purpose, other than giving bloodthirsty satisfaction to those who keep their own sins well hidden.' His voice grated. 'Esther would never recover from the horror of it and Malachi is already half crazed with grief and shame. I won't add to their burden.'

'I think Esther's coping better than Malachi because she believes in her heart that her daughter is somewhere safe,' Leah said softly.

'He is so ashamed he can't bear me near him. But the truth is I didn't want to marry Miriam because I loved her but because I desired her. None of this would have happened if I had waited until there was someone I could truly love. That is what Rebekah would have wanted for me.'

'It is what your grandmother would have wanted too, Tobiah.'

He took her hands in his and, like the breaking of a husk, she felt the last remnants of the protective wall that she had built around her heart give way. This gentle, reflective man, who was her son, evoked memories of Ulum, Daniel and Varinius who, each in their own way, had help redeem, by their simple goodness, all the pain she had suffered at the hands of others.

'What is it about you, Leah, that is being hidden from me?' Tobiah asked softly.

She was unprepared for his question and a feeling of dread clutched at her. She knew he had seen her fear and she clenched her fists, digging her nails deep into her palms as she fought down the desire to tell him the truth and claim him as her son.

She prevaricated. 'If you want me to tell you who Daniel's father was, then I shall,' she said.

There was a stillness about him that held her transfixed.

'I think you know, Leah, that's not what I want to hear. From the moment I found you lying across Daniel's grave and brought you to my home, I have felt a connection between us. That connection has to be something you, Ahava, Malachi and Esther haven't wanted me to discover.'

He lifted his wine cup and took a long drink before carefully replacing it on the table.

'I think that you are my mother. Are you?'

She brushed a strand of hair from across her face and breathed deeply.

'No, I am not your mother. My sister was your mother. But I am the woman who gave birth to you.'

His expression didn't change and she prepared herself for what he would ask next, and her heart broke. She knew if she revealed the truth it might drive him to despair because he would consider himself an abomination. Yet she could not lie to him.

'Who was my father,' he said softly.

'Before I tell you Tobiah, I need you to hear something else first.'

He was sitting very still and upright and she saw that his face had paled.

'I will listen to whatever you say, as long as it is the truth. And I shall know if it's not,' he said his voice low and even.

She closed her eyes whilst she gathered her thoughts and all her pain distilled into that moment.

'I want you to know, Tobiah, that when you were born and I looked into your tiny face I loved you and I always will. Leaving you with my sister, after I ran away from my husband, was a grief matched only by the death of Daniel. But I couldn't remain in Sychar then because I blamed your grandparents for what had happened to me. Nor could I take you with me, because I had no means of providing for you, but I knew Judith and Thomas would love you and look after you as though you were their own.'

She paused, her head lowered. He remained silent and unmoving, his eyes fixed steadily on her, forcing her to continue.

'Everyone in the village thought you were the child of my husband,' she said, lifting her head. 'Only your grandparents knew who your real father was.'

Overcome, she placed a hand across her mouth unable to speak the words he wanted to hear.

'Please remember how precious you were to them, Tobiah. I think your grandmother loved you more that she loved her own children.' She tried to smile but failed.

'Who was my father?' he said again, and this time his voice was demanding.

Her body trembled uncontrollably and her eyes pleaded as they met his.

She pressed her fingers to her lips again and drew a long, jagged breath rocking slightly as she did so.

'Your father was my brother Reuben. He raped me when I was thirteen years old'

He didn't move, nor did his face betray the wrenching torrent of emotion that swept through him.

She longed to hold him in her arms and tell him again that she loved him, but she knew he would be unable to bear her touch. Numbed by the enormity of what she had revealed she told him, bleakly, all had happened to her after that terrible day, until she returned to the village three years later to leave him with her sister. When she finished speaking she heard him take a long quiver of breath.

'I always felt my grandfather didn't like me because he was never comfortable with me,' he said, his voice flat. 'Sometimes it seemed as though he could hardly bear to have me near him. Now I know why. It was shame for what his son had done and for what I am. I think every time he looked at me he saw Reuben because I look like him, don't I, Leah?'

'Yes,' she whispered. 'You do look like him. But you are nothing like him at all. What he did was an evil act, but it has been redeemed in you. You have only ever brought joy and love to those who have known you. It was your grandfather's son who shamed him, not you.'

'I need time to think. I remember you clearly now. I remember you holding me tight before you left and how I cried for you after you had gone. I want to say I wish I had never found you and brought you to my home, but it wouldn't be true. My grandmother was at peace when she died because of you.'

They sat in silence for a while. Leah with her head bowed low and Tobiah with his hands clasped tightly in his lap.

'Are there any more secrets, Leah?' he asked softly.

Her heart lurched as she thought of the secret about her own father, that his beloved grandmother had carried for so many years, and she knew that now was not the time for it to be revealed.

'Yes, there is something else that you should know about and it concerns us both. But it will keep until we have mourned your grandmother and then we will talk again.'

She prepared herself for his demand that she tell him now. But he didn't. Instead he picked up his sleeping mat and blanket.

'I will see you in the morning,' he said, his voice flat and emotionless.

As he left she wrapped her arms around herself and rocked to and fro. And she thought she would never feel warm again

Chapter Twenty-Five

After a long, sleepless night Leah got up whilst it was still dark and lit the lamps, then she went to sit at the table, resting her head on her folded arms. As she became aware of a presence in the doorway she looked up to see Tobiah silhouetted in the pale light of the breaking dawn.

She raised a hand to her throat and her eyes followed him as he crossed the room. He looked tired and drawn as he sat down beside her and clasped both her hands in his. Her breathing became suspended as she waited for him to speak.

'I'm glad you told me the truth,' he said, gravely.

She sat up straight and sighed deep within herself.

'You were right, Leah, when you said you are not my mother. Nor was Reuben my father. Thomas, the man who raised me, loved me and taught me the scriptures at his knee and his craft as a potter, was my father. My mother was the woman who loved me and cradled me in her arms when I was hurt or frightened. She was the woman who tried to mend my broken toys, and bathed the grazes on my knees when I had fallen down. No matter what the circumstances of my conception, God blessed me with loving parents. I was their child and I have tried to be the man they would have wanted me to be.'

Leah said a silent prayer of gratitude and a feeling of overwhelming relief swept through her. For a long while neither of them spoke. It was Tobiah who broke the silence.

'There is no need for you to leave the village now. Stay and make your home here with me.' He tried to laugh but failed. 'I have already told you, I don't believe the reasons you gave me for wanting to leave Sychar.'

Unable to speak, she shook her head.

'Listen to me,' he said. 'Esther will need a friend now because the other women will go on gossiping about what has happened, for a long time to come, and some may shun her. But you are strong Leah, stronger than Esther. You can protect her from their malice by being by her side when they point a finger. And in time it will pass. The whisperings will stop and things will go on as before.'

He smiled and stroked the scar on her face. 'Daniel, your son, my brother, is buried here. And it is here in Sychar where you need to be.'

A gentle breeze wafted in through the open doorway, sending tiny pinpricks of light from the oil lamps dancing across the walls. Leah nodded her head and a feeling of peace and lightness flowed between them like the aftermath of a storm.

As the sun began to rise they joined the men, women and children, who had gathered in the synagogue. They had come to hear the Jewish rabbi, Jesus, preach once more before he left the village.

The room was full and the doors had been left open wide, so that those who had arrived late could stand outside to listen. There was a palpable excitement in the air. Even the small children were infected by it, laughing and pulling faces at their friends as they pushed and wriggled to free themselves from the restraining arms of their mothers.

Leah sat immersed in thought beside Esther, oblivious to the many curious stares from the women of the village and the sly, sideways looks of the men.

A village elder stood on the dais, along the wall facing the gathering, and his voice rang out in prayer and praise of God. Then he invited Jesus to come forward. As he stood and walked to the front of the crowd the eyes of everyone fixed on him and a soft murmur rippled, like a gentle tide. Then silence settled and the room filled with the power of his presence.

Never had they heard anyone preach with such eloquence or authority. He had not come to question the validity of the Law but to remind them that at its heart was mercy, and that true goodness was to be found in the spirit of charity and love, not the strict keeping of religious rules and regulations. The vision he gave them was of a God of compassion and forgiveness who could be known as a loving father and who would transform lives and restore hope. He was teaching a new understanding of God's will and their faces, lit by the warm glow from the candles, were set into deep lines of concentration. Even the children were stilled.

Tobiah turned to look at Malachi who was sitting on the carpet, cross-legged, in the row behind him, his head in his hands. As he sensed his eyes on him he looked up, his face so pain filled that instinctively Tobiah reached out to him and they clasped hands, whilst the men around them, moved to sympathy, averted their gaze

From the side of the room, where the women and small children were sitting, Esther watched her husband with hope stirring in her heart as his eyes, pleading for understanding, found hers. The look she gave to him was filled with such immeasurable tenderness and love that he knew they would find their way back from the dark place that had claimed them.

After the final prayer of blessing everyone began to leave. Leah remained until the last. She had pulled the emerald ring from her finger and it was lying in the closed palm of her hand. She hesitated a moment and then she crossed the floor to where one of Jesus' followers stood. Holding out her hand she uncurled her fingers. His face betrayed his shocked surprise as he looked down at what she was offering.

'The ring is mine to give,' she said softly. 'Sell it and use the money to help your master.'

He nodded his head once in acknowledgement and took the ring, placing it in the leather pouch hanging from his belt. With another nod towards her he turned to join his companions, who were making ready to continue on their journey to Galilee.

She remained for a few moments longer, standing in the shadows at the back of the room, breathing in the atmosphere; her spirit renewed and strengthened by her growing belief in the message of Jesus, and the love and mercy of God.

Silently she forgave all those who had harmed her. Then, as the last vestiges of her corrosive hatred for Marcellus and Aaron drained away, a great warmth and calm infused her being. She had loved both Daniel and Ulum and now her memories of them were freed to live at peace in her heart.

As she emerged into the sunlight, she stood watching the people of Sychar wending their way home. At the back of the large crowd Tobiah and Malachi walked beside each other, their heads close together as they talked. She hurried to catch up with Esther and slipped an arm around her waist.

'I think he, Jesus, is the Messiah that we have been waiting for,' Esther said softly.

Leah smiled and drew her closer.

Printed in Great Britain
by Amazon.co.uk, Ltd.,
Marston Gate.